THE
NYMPHOLEPTS

THE
NYMPHOLEPTS

Liam Hudson

JONATHAN CAPE
THIRTY BEDFORD SQUARE LONDON

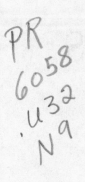
First published 1978
© 1978 by Liam Hudson

Jonathan Cape Ltd, 30 Bedford Square,
London wc1

British Library Cataloguing in Publication Data
Hudson, Liam
The nympholepts.
I. Title
823'.9'1F   PR6058. U/

ISBN 0-224-01616-4

Printed in Great Britain
by Ebenezer Baylis and Son Ltd
The Trinity Press, Worcester, and London

'NYMPHOLEPSY'

A state of desire or frenzy
for the unattainable, once
inspired in the male by young
women or nymphs.

'NYMPHOLEPTS'

Ones so inspired ...

January 21st

It has rained for a fortnight. I can think of nothing to say,
even to myself.

January 30th

'*A story has no beginning or end: arbitrarily one chooses that
moment of experience from which to look back or from which to
look ahead.*' It's precipitating there too, in *The End of the
Affair*. There's a hole in Graham Greene's umbrella, or in
his hero's at least. His bed-sit's on the wrong side of the
Common. Without bothering to leaf back, checking dates,
you know he was in his forties when that particular mood
of irritation struck him. Comfort, the wadding we forty-
year-olds cling to. 'The wrong memory,' he calls it, 'in the
wrong place or time.' A black January night, and a man
Greene hates slanting across a wide river of rain. And
facing you beside that first page of his, slanting into your
field of view from the left, a motto from Leon Bloy, that
looks like a good idea dented in translation from the
French : '*Man has places in his heart which do not yet exist,
and into them enters suffering in order that they may have
existence.*'

March 1st

Watery behind the blinds, the sun. A tiny shift in the
level of ambient light that stirs the pituitary gland. What
awaits me in my Bloy-spaces? The aches and pains of a
mature relationship? Heaven forbid.

March 9th

What the sun rekindles is hope. Last night, Penny and I went across the Park, and had a Greek supper together. She recovered some of her spontaneity for the occasion. There was not a trace of the bitter undertow I now take for granted.

When we got back to the flat and settled for the night — she in my bed and I on the sofa — it seemed that we had rediscovered some of the warmth that twins hold in store for each other, but rarely dispense. It was not to last, though. Rather than going to sleep, she wandered back into the sitting-room, sat beside me, and initiated one of our wrangles about the defects of my personality. Beneath a surface irritation, I've always drawn from these a gratification that's redolent of our adolescence, sitting together around a coal fire on a gusty autumn afternoon. She speaks from an assumed authority that's absolute. It's less a matter of picking holes here and there in an admittedly tattered fabric; more a celebration of the ascendency over me that she's enjoyed as long as I can remember.

Her central theme is my focuslessness. My role on these occasions is to grant the truth of what she's saying in general terms, but make clever arguments in extenuation. To her the roof beams, to me the filigree.

That she is in principle right and I am in principle wrong is itself a principle never questioned. What's at stake is the drawing of the boundary between our two domains : the precise extent to which I will let her exercise her sovereignty in overruling my better judgment over matters of detail. It's the grey area in the relation of political boss to executive officer, the world over.

As usual, her onslaught last night had three prongs.

The first addresses my failure to hold down a clearly identifiable job. I'm something in the City; that she acknowledges. But it's a source of resentment to her that she never quite knows what. Also that, whatever it is, it only occupies part of my time. In extenuation, I remind her that I've a flair for innovation that's in the past been considered valuable; and when my nerve is strong, I try out on her the labels I sometimes find attached to me: 'consultant', 'our trouble-shooter' — even 'change agent'.

Though offered in inverted commas and in the appropriate spirit of self-deprecation, these categories invariably meet a hail of scorn, and I only occasionally attempt them. Her position is in any case complex. At first sight she appears to say that instead of hiring myself out around the merchant banks, I should have carved out a real career for myself. As heart specialist or barrister. But to counter-attack on such an assumption is an error. I learnt this long ago. You walk into the right cross that follows the left hook. For she then claims that although I'm the clever one, there's a deeper artistic vein to my temperament to which I'm continually unfaithful. Rather than dabbling round the edge of the arts, I should have had the nerve to plunge straight in. A painter. Better still, a photographer: the Cartier-Bresson of my generation. She is now impregnable, because she's driven home the insinuation that my analytical intelligence is superficial; and should I show signs, argumentatively, of chucking up my life in the City and becoming a photographer full-time, she's then free with the news that it's too late — that I'm too old and dog-eared for such *jeux d'esprit*.

How stately our quarrels are: as determinate as copulation. But my job constitutes only the first focus of her dissatisfaction. More pressing is her irritation at my failure to put down roots. There's this flat, furnished with loving care. But I'm always relieved to leave it. There's the room poor Mother warms for me each Christmas. There's Penny's spare room. But none of these is home.

The nearest approximation is the Voisins'. I've often wondered quite what its hold is. Partly, I suppose, the light. Perched on its cliff top, it looks straight out into the pearly haze that obsessed Monet and de Staël. There's a clash of knives and forks and a hum of talk as you walk down through the back-streets of Trouville to the quay that's as reassuring as any noise in the world. If the mood takes you, you can wander across and look at the beautiful people in Deauville too.

The real claims, though, are archaeological. Literally, in that the house stands on a fossil bed, and the beaches are littered in winter with the petrified remains of plants and animals that last breathed in and out a hundred million years ago. But metaphorically too. It's a place that compels the reconstruction of the past. As the coast crumbles, it takes with it the block houses that the Germans built against Eisenhower. The house was itself requisitioned as a billet, and its wooden floors are still scarred and scratched with Teuton hob-nails. It sobers me to think that the basement where I brew my coffee in the morning once echoed, well within my lifetime, to the oaths of sleepy German batmen; and down the road, against a wall, groups of Frenchmen were shot to foster docility in those left alive.

Like a decaying friendship, the house shows awful new sights of subsidence each time I go there. Yet it's inspired enough faith in the Voisins for them to provide it with a new roof, so I suppose they expect it to last as long as we do. Even the house's furnishings remind you of the succession of generations, the precipitation of their taste laid down, decade on decade. The topmost straight from Maison Marie Claire; good taste off the peg, the influence of Marguerite. Beneath that, remnants of the ghastly French chic of the immediately post-war years; utility materials tricked out in black and gold to look gracious — a cocktail trolley now pressed into service as a television table, odious multicoloured glasses still used for apéritifs. Beneath that, a more serious contribution: evidence of someone, perhaps Voisin Père, who took a sustained interest in Spain; Spanish dining room chairs, purgatorial to sit on, flimsy Spanish wrought iron everywhere, a massively wooden dining table, Spanish in its inspiration, but several centuries newer than it pretends to be. And beneath that again, evidence of a taste genuinely discriminating. Whose I don't know, but still as strong in the house as the smell of drains: massive provincial armoires and cupboards, here and there carved cherry-wood panels, and the remnants of authentically massive brass work. Upstairs, in the rooms the Voisins use at weekends, Habitat beanbags to sit on; but down in the body of the house, amidst pink and grey flowered wallpaper, antique chairs that collapse under the least weight, formal beds, and pillows that hit the neck like a sandbag.

Not even the doom of my last visit there with Beth-the-Social-Work has spoilt the place for me. Like Penny, Beth was alert to the lack of commitment at the centre of what she called my life-style. She wasn't being censorious, but it was visibly depressing her, almost as if struggling with the decision to marry a man with an irreversibly degenerative disease.

Far from being depressing, in fact, that holiday yielded one of those cameos around which one yearns to write a novel.

On her last day, I took Beth round by bus to Le Havre, and tried to explain to her, while we waited for her ferry, why it moved me : the worst-devastated port in Europe, all those priceless mediaeval houses now replaced in reinforced concrete. I took her to look at Perret's town hall, a concrete classic, but that didn't reach her either. We then had our picnic outside Nouvelles Galeries, on a bench between the old commercial dock and the war memorial.

Like the town, the memorial actually seems to say something about death and renewal. A clumsy block topped in human figures ; the whole thing, even the figures, fabricated like the town out of building blocks. And the pediment covered in names ; tiny, gold-lettered. By any standards there are a lot of them, and they're supplemented at the bevelled corners by addenda from Algeria and Vietnam.

Afterwards, when her letter arrived, letting me know about the lecturer in anthropology young enough to be my son, it occurred to me that my name might be added to those on the memorial. In chalk, a small and respectfully placed item of graffiti, rather than in the full legitimacy of gold.

A sentimental touch to set my sister's teeth on edge. She takes it as a reflection on herself, this failure of mine to marry. She wouldn't welcome a sister-in-law. I know that, and she knows that I know. And to that extent her position is flawed. But she genuinely hates the pattern my romances follow : surges of enthusiasm that fail to culminate even in a magisterial row. That simply ebb away. More than that : she hates the extent to which women dominate my processes of thought. Instead of marrying, recurringly, cyclically, I'm intrigued by marriage. Like the natural-born observer everywhere, I hover around what obsesses me, trying to plumb its meaning rather than taking part : watching, rather than allowing the social mechanisms we've evolved to dull obsession's edge, to blur and blind. (And I'm unrepentant. Whenever I tell myself that if I'm to understand marriage I must marry, I point out to myself a fact : that no one is more baffled by marriage than the married themselves. Observers observe because they're too alarmed to take part ; participants participate to avoid true knowledge of what they're participating in. Our two great trades routes towards eventual numbness, with all manner of wobbly sheep-tracks along the slopes in between.)

If my interest in the marriageable and the married were lecherous, Penny could accept it. Tiresome, embarrassing even ; but part of the natural order. But for an unmarried man in his forties to view women as the centre of an abiding fascination, as the nodes around which his whole imaginative world arranges itself — this she deems unnatural. It's an awkwardness between sister and self that would smooth itself away if I were willing to dissimulate — I know that ; if, like a well-adjusted executive, I could pretend to ogle my friends' wives and to fantasise about sixteen-year-olds without their clothes. But it's just that pretence that I've always been unwilling to make ; it's a sacrifice of principle that lies outside my moral range. So Penny and I have to reach a more precarious compromise. For polemic purposes, she denounces my fascination out of hand. But while it's marriage that brings her ridicule to the boil, it's also the theme that betrays in her an underlying softening of will. Once it's broached, I know I'm free to deploy whatever diversionary argument I can muster. She's willing to watch while I dance, permitting me to defend my preoccupation as the root from which stem all the more beautiful of civilisation's products; healthy in a bachelor of any age, and preferable to pederasty.

It's a track replete with branch lines and sidings, and when on song, I exploit them all. This last time, I remembered to remind Penny of the Duke of Omnium who was half in love with every woman merely for her womanhood; a man who succumbed to petticoats unconsciously. While she disapproves of Trollope instinctively, she has never formulated a good reason for rejecting him. So instead of specific rebuttal, she expresses a generalised contempt, accepting my efforts the while as the tokens of devotion and dependence that in truth they are.

Courtesy of the *Sunday Times*, I found to my delight, last night, that I had a new diversionary curlicue to explore. It suddenly struck me, with the force of revelation, that the whole of philosophy springs from the mystery inherent in the opposition of the sexes. 'Mind and body' is of its essence an erotic problem: the relation of bodily movement and behavioural sign to sensation and to fantasy. And so is 'other minds': the fascination that grips us when we try to imagine ideas that lie behind the eyes of someone we love. The Anglo-Saxon preoccupation with evidence: nothing more nor less than our anxiety at the gap between the total knowledge of the other that our love demands and the sketchy clues on which we're forced in practice to depend. The lover's jealous and maddening doubt. The whole of formal knowledge a transposition and echo of sexual knowledge. Even the conundrums of ethics fit into the scheme somewhere: our puzzlement that

14

beauty should be given to some while the rest of us do without.

I could concede that professional philosophers don't write articles about the female form ; but even this was grist to my dialectical mill. It's known that all great philosophers are celibates ; what more likely, then, that philosophical inquiry itself should be an onanistic denial and defence against the erotic impulse?

Uncharacteristically, Penny was impressed. She'd been reading about Bertrand Russell, and had noticed that he disliked women whilst chasing them compulsively. He seemed to hate them, but needed to get inside them, as if they were shellfish. With that, she was happy for the second time to go off to bed.

March 11th

Titles for the novel I couldn't write to save my life : 'Transparencies'. The psyche revealed, layer on layer. An amateur photographer's pun. Better still : 'Grave Doubt' — a pun for a necrophiliac private eye.

March 12th

Round for a meal with Penny. Perce had made himself scarce ; but the Mulloys were there too. Boomer went on at length about central heating ; when he and Ess moved house, he'd felt inspired to install his own. There's a pride in him about being the kind of engineer who can lever RSJs into place. The practical man : but lacunae open up between the theory and the deed. He'd bought up surplus radiators as an *Exchange and Mart* job lot, and used some patent pipe to link them : coated steel that's half the price of copper, but leaks when the water gets hot.

After supper, we tramped round to have a look. Ess is being exemplarily forbearing, but you can see from the wreckage that the system sprang its leaks after she put up her curtains, not before. They've had two full-scale floods, and Boomer's greasy fingerprints are on door handles and paint work. Although the furniture's polished, the surfaces are covered in films of builder's lime. You'd expect Ess to nag, but I caught no trace of it. Rather, she seems to construe the whole episode as an outrage the Fates have perpetrated at her husband's expense. There's even a hint that they should have more respect for his professional qualifications. For a woman by nature tidy, it's a feat of solidarity you can only admire. Whatever the wounds, they're not being allowed to show.

Penny told me on the way home that when she and Perce called round on Boxing Day, the house was freezing, and Ess had entertained them to glasses of sherry in a frame tent erected in the midst of her sitting room, flaps pulled down, and heat provided by Calor gas. A tidy woman married to an untidy man.

March 15th

Boomer's plumbing raises the question of what married couples see in each other. Sometimes it's a mystery, even after the event — as with Penny and Perce. With the Mulloys, you can sense the nature of the bond, but can't put it into words. There's also the puzzle of why pairs get along together as foursomes. With Boomer and Ess,

16

Penny and Perce, I can think of no explanation other than loneliness.

When I first met them, the only vivid impression I had of the Mulloys was Ess's hair. An orange-red halo. A dayglo extravaganza. I've noticed that women whom God has given this one preponderant libidinal advantage are rarely beautiful or even pretty. Also that their personalities, once you locate them, can seem something of an anticlimax. This was heightened for me in Ess's case by the note of formality she strikes. You're aware of her clothes ; their quality and the care she takes of them, more aware of her clothes than the person inside them. The overall effect is one of bourgeois propriety rather than seduction. Someone who goes silently on her daily round. Certainly not humming or singing out loud.

To my knowledge she and Boomer never bicker. On the contrary, they conspire together to create an impression of unity. Exactly the kind of woman, exactly the kind of marriage, to get on Penny's nerves — or so I would have thought. When she and Perce moved in round the corner, I introduced them, without expecting it to take ; yet manifestly it has. Why am I so surprised?

Primarily, I think, because of Penny's life-long dedication to sexual warfare. Since earliest teens, she's been magnetically attractive to men ; which is the same as saying, I suppose, that she has a lasting commitment to attract them. As far back as I can recollect, there's been that steady stream of men of all ages, all hues, all degrees of desirability. And paying court to someone who, all her life, has been short and plump. Vivacious, but scarcely better than plain. When a girl, she could hint that she was for ever on the brink of falling in love ; yet never quite did so. But more and more, it's the frisson of personal

17

attraction that preoccupies her. At first, the curiosity of the explorer, mapping out the extent of her domain, but now, jaded with success, an appetite for matters more martial.

Another cameo. This time, one for the budding biographer rather than the novelist manqué. Penny as an undergraduate, attending a sherry party at her brother's college – the Master's Lodge. Detectably, she favours the traces of Persian in our background : tightly curled black hair, later liberally flecked with premature grey ; a complexion that tans quickly, and looks remarkable when set against the spots and pastiness of the middle-class English maid. Without effort, she monopolises the attention of the Master, a scholarly and somewhat rheumatic philologist. Elsewhere the deference of the 1950s reigns : someone is trying to talk to the Master's wife about rowing while the rest of us fidget with our glasses and long for half an hour to pass. The Master, though, has succumbed. Without warning, he performs a head stand in the midst of his own drawing room, solely because Penny has expressed doubt that he could. Coins shower from his trouser pockets, and a lonely half-crown rolls across the parquet to end at his horrified wife's feet. Ostensibly, Penny is all innocent delight, but already there's a steadier gleam in her eye too : the distant rumble of cannon and the crumbling of citadel walls.

She was at her peak then, though she would not have dreamt it at the time. University to her was a depressing extension of school. Real life would begin when she got into the theatre. And it's true, she does have a talent, but it's not a momentous one. She was more convincing in the flesh than she would ever be across the footlights. Faced with competition from those washed-out, empty-eyed professionals who burst into life as the lights go up, she was at a disadvantage she could never overcome.

Perhaps that's what led her to marry the preposterous Perce. Perce whom she'd met at a party.

A second biographer's cameo: the day Penny brought Perce home. Perce with his crinkled hair, carefully combed, and twill trousers creased. She offers him to her nearest and dearest with an airy gesture, as if he were a new pedal-bin to fit under her sink. Self-contained in his armchair, Perce keeps his own counsel: he seems immune to Penny, while she discusses him as if he weren't there.

Dad, bemused, asks Perce about his means of livelihood, market research. The Almighty must have had Perce in mind when He fashioned that particular commercial niche; it fits him wonderfully. An industry where it's *de rigueur* to adopt a mid-Atlantic accent, yet where Perce can carve out an ersatz reputation for sincerity by retaining a trenchantly Scottish one.

After half an hour, our parents stumble away towards the kitchen, thunderstruck, leaving the three of us to chat. Penny talks across Perce to me, still ignoring him. She passes the time by parodying the intimacies that Perce sees fit to breathe into her ear: 'Alone at last', and 'How can I have lived without you'. An exact recreation of a noise that's at once sugary and self-righteous: puff pastry stuffed with grit.

Beyond a shadow of doubt, Penny is not in love with him; nor can she find him physically attractive. My guess at the time, stumbling away in my parents' wake, is that she caught herself speaking stage Cockney once too often, and picked on Perce because he was so remote from any notion of theatrical glamour.

In the kitchen afterwards, my father seeks the solace of

philology and puns. He passes feeble jokes about pennies and purses from hand to hand. Also the idea that she's drawn to him because, at school in France, she'd been known dismissively as '*La perse*'. My mother cries; and on reflection that still seems to me the more apposite reaction of the two.

So much of their relationship comes down to voices. Penny's stage voices and imitations; and Perce's 'real' voices, all of which are unbelievable. All except one: the voice he uses when talking to Ess. She seems to like him and speaks to him with a care that sets him visibly at ease. Briefly, puzzled and defenceless, he's like a man emerging from fugue; and for those moments, his intonation contains scarcely a trace of Scottish.

For the rest, Perce is compelled to present himself in terms that invite disbelief. Yet another cameo. Perce standing in front of his sitting room fireplace, announcing that he must go on a trip. Penny does not pretend to believe him; no one could. But it's a cameo centrally placed amidst the mysteries of their marriage, because it's during these absences of Perce's that the grosser of her indiscretions occur. The ones from which all semblance of festivity is stripped away, and that leave behind them a graveyard chill. Someone with a smattering of psycho-analysis would assume that she has Perce's connivance; even that there's some profound satisfaction there for him, and that he colludes with her so that they take place. But so much for theory: I live close to them, and if forced to offer a diagnosis, would have to admit that I can't tell. Some days my judgment swings one way; some days the other.

Today, for the first time in my life, I spoke to Ess about her job. She was reticent. At first, I put this down to defensiveness at having to work in an office, having once played the piano. But was wrong. It's that she likes to keep the Bureau separate. The company of intelligent women is something she enjoys ; and she talks about her dealings with developers and builders with a warmth I wouldn't have foreseen. Over the years, she's grown wary, and can now spot a fast one before it's pulled. But without those cheerful knaves to thwart, I'm sure her pleasure would have begun to pall.

I still can't grasp how she and Penny get on so well. I would expect Ess to be alarmed, and Penny to find Ess unsatisfactorily lady-like. Their clothes, for instance. Ess's, decidedly expensive, while Penny grabs whatever comes to hand. She looks like a pirate, and takes vociferous objection to women who lavish patience on what they look like. Such differences usually cut deep : but in this case offer no obstacle at all. Mutual suspicion there may be ; but if so, it's firmly in check.

Afterwards, I went along to watch Boomer and Perce play squash, and a pretty pair of self-portraits they provide. On the way, Perce held forth about brake linings, while Boomer and I listened in silence. Perce kits himself out in all the right gear, and wields his Maxply absolutely according to the textbook : all hard-muscled and bouncy. While Boomer stands there in an unpleasant football jersey and moves in a lumbering shamble. By rights, Perce should dissect him, but it's Boomer who wins. Perce hits the ball crisply to where the book says he should hit it ; Boomer hits it hard to where Perce can't reach it. Boomer has an ill-focused flair for the game, while Perce has not a scrap: none of which prevents Perce from treating Boomer like a beginner who's in continual need of advice.

We all had supper afterwards, and in their own ways Ess and Penny caricature themselves in their food as vividly as their husbands do on court. Ess's idea of a staple diet is bread and cheese, black olives, and gin and tonic. The quality's excellent, but the tone is frugal. Like the table you eat it off: scrubbed pine. And the room you eat it in: white paint, scraped wood, and a few scattered ornaments, carefully placed, but bleak. That's not Penny's style at all. There is something vulgar and Cordon Bleu-ish about Penny's meals, as there is about our whole family, I suppose. She'll decide to provide Lobster Thermidor, as though we're going out to a flashy, slightly second-rate restaurant; and she'll do it with gusto, with trimmings. Almost with names on little cards. Not just Lobster Thermidor, but five courses, cooking all day when the spirit moves her, and well. Penny *cooks*; Ess serves up food that's already prepared by someone else or raw.

Round the table, a perfect sociogram: four worlds of experience and the bonds between them. When you examine the diagram, you find something unexpected. For when they're together as a foursome, it's Penny who's the hub of activity and noise. But look at the sociogram and what do you see? That the hub is not Penny after all, but Ess. She is the only member of the foursome with access to the other three: to Boomer, of course; to Penny; and in an unobtrusive way to Perce. Penny's cut off from Perce; and Boomer is only connected to him in a superficial way. It's Perce who's the isolate, linked in only via Ess.

22

To be up-to-date, I've got to include myself in the pattern too. The observer no less than the observed. The participant who has no one to share with, so commits his perceptions to faulty prose. A narrator who talks to himself, and who's tied by Oedipal bonds of steel to one of the other four. An amateur sociologist when things go smoothly, and half-a-psychologist when in the toils! (Perhaps all narrators are talking to themselves — addicted to glimpses of the sea caught over characters' shoulders and between trees.)

March 30th

Disconcerting to find that I like the pictures in Berger's book about the nude that he's put there to disapprove of. Lely's Nell Gwynne, and some of the pin-ups. Berger says that it's the sight of the body as an object that encourages its use as an object. But there are objects and objects. Some are status symbols; others are reservoirs of light. (And others still are both at the same time. People likewise.)

An absurd conversation this morning with two go-getters who have been hawking gas boilers around the Common Market. At their instigation, someone in their firm has paid out £100,000 for political services — as far as I can tell, for oiling wheels that don't need oiling.

One's middle-aged and gritty, the other younger and smooth. They present themselves as the new breed of Anglo-Saxon, willing to sup with the Devil if sup they must. Wheels have been oiled, and wheels have turned; but no contracts have yet materialised. My honest Brits have been taken for a long Byzantine ride. It's just dawned on them that there exists no courtroom in the world where they can stand up and claim justice. And even if it did, that they would damn themselves out of their own mouths as perverters of the free market and fools. Patiently, I told them about Lockheed. They knew the story as well as I did, but had assumed that it could not apply to people like themselves.

April 9th

A good bracketful: '(*You are not bad, you are merely unhappy, the bathtub murderer is "sick", the Dead End Kid is a problem child, poor Hitler is a paranoiac, and that dirty fornication in a hotel room, why, that, dear Miss Sargent, is a "relationship"*) ...'

And a useful turn of phrase: ' ... *a sense of artistic decorum that like a hoity-toity wife was continually showing one's poor biography the door*'. Obliquely, it brings back the only interesting conversation I've overheard in twenty-five years of snooping. (An inveterate eavesdropper on buses and trains, I must have caught snatches of 10,000 or more, which proves there's nothing in the theory of positive reinforcement.) At the time, this one took me so much by surprise, I forgot to write it down. Comfortably, a young lady with frizzy blonde curls was setting a young lady with frizzy black ones a conundrum. 'Why would we rather have an affair with the actor who plays the handsome surgeon on television than with the real surgeon, just as handsome?' Black Friz had all sorts of suggestions: 'Because the actor would be better than the surgeon at pretending he had a mind.' 'Because the actor might have met Angela Rippon.' 'Because the actor isn't really there.'

But Blonde Friz would accept none of these, though all were close. The correct answer, she deemed, was 'because the actor offers fiction while the surgeon offers fact — and fact is an aphrodisiac, by definition.' When they got off, they were trying to work out whether the surgeon could overtake the actor by pretending to be an actor pretending to be a surgeon. And whether the actor would still succeed if he refused to let you believe it was the television surgeon you were going to bed with. If he insisted on being himself. It was a number 22 bus, and they got off at Sloane Square.

May 10th, 11th, 12th

The moment's come to stitch some of the events of the last three weeks together.

The first ripples of disaster reached me on Wednesday afternoon. Ironically, spring had just arrived : the kind of day on which you thank God you're not working abroad, and can still enjoy the English phantasmagoria of village pubs and pints on the green.

Boomer told me afterwards that it was the same in Paris, where he had gone on one of his business trips. He'd spent the early evening wandering in St-Germain-des-Prés, and then lay for hours in a small hotel bedroom, windows wide open, watching that same sunset throwing light on the leaves of the tree in the courtyard, and on the stucco of the building opposite. Very pastoral ; he said that he could have been in a small provincial town. Nevers, say. For the first time in years the clatter of arrangements subsided, and he lay with his head empty, as he often had as a boy.

I had just vanquished a circular about take-over bids, and was heading for a cup of coffee across the street, when I came across a forlorn young policeman standing in our lobby. He'd just been turned away by our Miss Brown. She explained that he had been asking for a Dr Brown, and that she'd told him we had no Dr Brown. She'd probably gone on to tell him that the only Brown we did have was herself, *Miss* Brown. What she had not volunteered was that we had a Dr Bowen. Myself. Ostensibly, she was protecting me from fuss; more covertly she was testing the special relationship she's woven around me, to see whether I'd the moral energy to break out.

For once she'd miscalculated, and I went to his rescue. I'll pay for my ungratefulness; but it'll be some time yet before I can give my mind to the niceties of fence-mending with Miss Brown.

Perce had had an accident somewhere down in Sussex: he had driven his car into a tree, and was dead. And so too was his passenger, a young man as yet unidentified. The police needed Penny, and needed help in naming the young man.

In fiction, most bodies seem to identify themselves automatically, and in accordance with this convention Perce had mutely named himself with his bank card. Similarly, fictional friends and next-of-kin meet death with decisive telephone calls and journeys so quick that they avoid description. But what I then entered, trying to do my best by sister and brother-in-law, was not fiction but burlesque. Every misalignment of detail that could occur, did.

The police had gone to Penny's house, but found no one. She did not get home till much later. However, her neighbour remembered me and the name of my firm. But in the panic, I failed to grasp what the bobby in our lobby had said : where I should go and what I had to do. And by the time I'd realised this, he was nowhere to be seen. Of the two local police stations, I chose the wrong one; but the sergeant on duty took pity, and undertook to ring round. The answer : the bodies of Perce and his passenger had been taken to Brighton.

By the time I got to Brighton police station, it was almost eight o'clock. After some fumbling, my second sergeant reached the view that I had been sent in pursuit of the wrong bodies. The brace he had on his books were an elderly couple called Ramage, who'd met their Maker by colliding with a coach on the outskirts of Burgess Hill. Anxiety at this point transformed itself into the first warning of migraine. It would take some time, the sergeant said, to sort out where my bodies were. Perhaps it would be a good idea if I went and had a meal. He was attempting to be conciliatory.

The first place I came to was a hotel, and once the spell was broken, haste seemed pointless : Perce was dead and refrigerated. I could identify him as well tomorrow morning as I could tonight. In terms of his eternal soul or mine, a good night's rest was neither here nor there. I rang the police station, and the sergeant told me, with the air of a tricky investigation brought to a close, that the deceased were to be found thirty miles away cross-country in Tunbridge Wells.

I had a decent supper, booked in, went up to my room, had a shower, and was on the point of rolling between the sheets to watch television for half an hour, when I remembered Penny. She might at any moment come into the house, and be turned loose, with goodness knows what garbled message, to search the South of England for Perce as I was doing.

In the end I got her. She'd just walked in ; and I found myself telling my sister, buoyant with two good days away from home and away from Perce, that she would spend the rest of her days away from him. That he was dead but that I was coping, and not to be distraught. She must go round and spend the night with Ess. She made no reply at all. Thinking that she might have collapsed, I rang off, and rang back. After more attempts, the operator opined that the receiver was off its hook. I tried Ess but got nothing. It then struck me for the first time that despite all those years of mutual hostility, Penny would be grief-stricken. Also that given the least excuse, she would unload her grief on me. Right or wrong, I'd no choice but to make a reparative dash through the night to Tunbridge Wells, and find Perce on my own.

But easier envisaged than achieved. It was now 11.30, and it took time to find a taxi firm willing to send someone so far afield: across the South Downs and into the wilderness beyond.

In the end, one relented ; and we set off together, the driver and I, into the pitch dark and roughly north-east. The blind led the blind. He had no inkling where Tunbridge Wells was ; nor where Kent was in relation to Sussex. Nor, I began to suspect from his driving, where left was in relation to right. We arrived a little before 2 a.m. But it is one thing to arrive in a sleeping town ; another to find its police station. We careered through from one side of the town to the other several times before finding our goal. It was the right place, but the wrong time. I couldn't visit the mortuary until nine the next morning. So at the duty sergeant's suggestion, I spent the rest of the night in a cell. My sciatic nerve was stabbing, foretaste of Penny's rage. But a cell is a protected spot — prisoners often say that. And I fell to musing about Perce's companion, and about what they'd been doing together, late in the evening, in the midst of the Ashdown Forest. What could possibly have happened that would cause cautious Perce to smash violently enough to kill them both?

Having mused, it struck me with the force of revelation that Perce was homosexual. For all his purring down the telephone, there was something deeply antipathetic in Perce to the feminine principle; a Calvinistic sense of shame that generalised itself to cover every manifestation of the spirit that was tender or nurturative. It must have been a spasm of passion that had transformed his normally sedate driving into a headlong dash beyond all prudence or caution.

It's curious how blind one can be; how the familiar can obscure the obvious. Yet obvious it was. Not just the conspicuousness of Perce's masculinity: there was so much that now fitted into shape. His shiftiness for example. I'd always assumed, idly, that this was just part of his profile, almost in the sense that his nose was. But it was shiftiness with a purpose; that of creating unaccountable time in which to forage. Even more telling was his immunity to Penny. She could not reduce him to rubble because his profoundest appetites were directed elsewhere. He could have children just as he could play squash and ski, as part of the disguise behind which his true needs lay hidden.

This realisation brought with it affection and even respect. He'd pulled a fast one. The butt, all these years, of Penny's ridicule, shoved by collective conspiracy into the position of isolate, he'd had the last laugh. She could not possibly have guessed. Had the truth dawned, she would have used it remorselessly: the most sharply barbed weapon she could wish for. Their bargain had been an idiosyncratic one, and scarcely comfortable; but with it Perce had brought a freedom that none of us had imagined he possessed.

With this thought, I dozed, and dreamt about cadavers in chests of drawers. By 8.45, I was on my way to the mortuary to face a real cadaver in a real chest of drawers. And as the attendant pulled it open for me, on rollers like a filing cabinet, there indeed was Perce. In the course of a lifetime, you peer into a drawer many thousands of times, looking for socks, or documents. To peer in and see the effigy of someone you've known for years, whose tone of voice is embedded in your memory, is unnerving — or at least I found it so. That it was Perce, there was not the slightest doubt. There was a massive contusion on his temple, but otherwise it was Perce as I knew him. To the life, one might almost say.

I was just getting back into the police car, when I remembered Perce's passenger and the need to identify him too. I mentioned this to the constable; and together we went back into the building. After a little rummaging with lists, another refrigerated drawer was pulled open and I was beckoned over to have a look. Inside, I found myself staring not at a young man, but at Ess.

Apart from household pets, and horrified glances backstage in the local butcher's shop, my experience of this particular transformation has until now been nil. I certainly didn't feel what decent people are meant to feel: horror, disbelief — helpless ransacking of the imagination in search of some explanation of the inexplicable. In a matter of fact way, I simply felt that I'd been dealt the wrong card. A rule had been broken. It was not until I was on the train, halfway back to Victoria, that I laid any plan about getting hold of Boomer. I spent the whole afternoon on the phone, tracing his steps from one office to another through most of the bureaucracies of Western Europe. In desperation, I even rang our embassy in Paris and threw myself on their charity, only to be snubbed by a young woman who sounded as though she'd left Roedean the week before. Every twenty minutes or so, I came to with a start, realising that Ess was the person who had the information I so badly needed ; and just as mechanically lapsed back into the further realisation that she was no longer a source I could use.

In the end, Boomer solved my problem for me. He'd rung his office about an arrangement that had gone wrong ; and as an afterthought his secretary told him that I had rung. He would not have bothered, still, had he not tried to ring Ess the night before, got no reply, and had an uneasiness in his mind that something was wrong ; that Penny was ill or that Ess's father had died. I told him it was worse by far.

It is only rarely that you have to tell someone over the telephone that their spouse is dead. I had done it twice within the space of a few hours ; and was alarmed by the difference between the two undertakings. Ringing Penny, I'd the sense, despite the unchallengeable intimacy that exists between us, of reaching across a void : of trying to present myself as a messenger who's less than completely alien — and knowing, making the attempt, that I was failing. Penny's experience of Perce's death and mine are light years apart, and my sympathy for her is bound to seem that of an outsider. Her silence was a fitting commentary, I suppose, on the wretchedness of my performance. With Boomer, by comparison half a stranger, I experienced no distance: I could speak to him of Ess as though I were speaking to myself. And Boomer, God knows how many miles away in a phone booth in Brussels, caught this intimacy of understanding. I could tell him what had happened and where: that she'd obviously gone out for a spin in the country with Perce; and for some reason as yet unexplained they had swung off what was apparently an empty road and into a tree. Both were dead when help first arrived. Dead, I found myself telling Boomer, but not disfigured.

My next task was to trace Penny. She's gone to earth at Henley. Her impulse had been to gather her daughters to her, and go straight down there in the middle of the night, dragging our terrified parents from their bed by her hooting and knocking. It's a reflex that would have been intelligible to me if she'd ever found solace there, or the house stood for her as a haven. But she hasn't, and it doesn't. Yet who cares? If you've spent your life wound into the workings of your twin sister's psyche, an element of familiarity enters that can sometimes seem close to tedium. Even in times of crisis. Or perhaps then especially.

Caught up in a lightning strike of air traffic control staff and an unexplained diversion to Birmingham, Boomer stepped across the threshold of my flat just before lunch the next day. The journey had taken nineteen hours, and left him haggard. But within minutes we were immersed in inquests and coroners, and the precise causes of death. And as our supply of specifics began to run out, he set off on a seemingly inexhaustible excursion into reminiscence.

Sitting there in my kitchen, clutching his mug of coffee, he looked like a farmer; a man who'd made a good living selling farm machinery, say. It's only the stuttering shifts of his attention from topic to topic that remind you that he's made a rather less than good living doing something a little different.

To begin with, he'd lurch without detectable preface from inquiries about skid-marks and the siting of the fatal tree, to the dreams he and Ess had had on their last night shared. Frantically, he was rehearsing all those respects in which he suspected himself of inadequacy. At first, it all concerned Ess directly; but as the day wore on, he scanned more and more widely, going back to his own childhood, and to any moment in his past when he'd discovered a crucial element lacking in his own make-up.

Like religious broadcasts and bits of poetry scattered here and there in running prose, other people's dreams are one of the imagination's products I normally prefer to skip. But in this case, the chance to insinuate myself retrospectively into the midst of Ess's marriage was a privilege I found obscurely reassuring.

On that last night, they'd both woken in a sweat, as though they'd flu. Both had been dreaming that they were levitating, flying; and both had been flying along the course of rivers. In Ess's case, a proper river, the size of the Cherwell; in his, more a mountain stream. He'd been uneasy; but Ess had enjoyed her trip, a floatingly pleasant sensation that might resolve itself into something more specific, but in all probability would not.

Retailing this, Boomer sat there opposite me, a large Victorian house with its side torn away, all its domestic arrangements exposed for passers-by to see. He went on, rambling, to talk about Ess's habitual guardedness; and the odd contradiction that although the prospect of intimacy always seemed to alarm her, once the brink was crossed, she was at her ease, and in no hurry to return. Like the fear of stepping out of a brightly illuminated porch into the dark : in one sense alarming ; in another, as natural as shutting your eyes.

Boomer nagged away at this dissonance he sensed between them. He felt he'd been useful to her, hustling her across these thresholds of the imagination that she'd found so daunting, but lacking her eventual composure — her willingness to linger in the dark, and peer into the shadows. And he wanted to talk about the ways in which their relationship had perplexed him. He was not eulogising exactly, but plotting out the features of a landscape that struck him as special, and into which he had obtruded a flaw.

For the first time, he spoke to me about Ess's earlier marriage. She'd married and given up the piano more or less simultaneously. More strictly, she'd married on the rebound from the piano, and had done so impulsively, and with ineptitude. She'd fallen in love with an aspiring painter : one Vic Plamenetz. And they were married within a matter of weeks. According to Boomer, she could scarcely have made a worse choice. Vic exuded that malign quality, 'promise'. He flirted furiously with any male who came within reach, but was prevented by some unspecified psychological obstruction from doing much work. And, in his relation with Ess, was jealous. Initially it was jealousy about the level of accomplishment she'd reached : she had been a better pianist than he was a painter. But rapidly it became sexual. He suspected her every move, and was driven into a frenzy of mortification by every attention or glance.

Now Ess is not everyone's taste, but glances and attentions there were bound to be ; and for every attention there was a row. Other people's rows are banal, almost as a matter of definition ; but there seems to have been something more banal about theirs than most : wholly one-sided, with the Byronic Victor clattering round their flat, eventually banging his tousled head against walls and floor, while Ess did her frightened best to reassure and assuage.

Bad enough, you'd have thought ; but to confound her folly, Ess conceived. How Vic's endeavours in bed with Ess meshed together with those he was making in other directions, I do not know, and won't speculate. But I'd already gathered from my indiscreet sister that while Ess quite enjoyed whatever sex there was, she knew nothing of practical significance about birth control ; while Victor saw any such technical intervention as a barrier to the spiritual consummation that brought each row to an end.

Tragically — I hadn't realised this — the child was born defective. Ess managed as best she could ; caring for her baby, and caring for Victor in his conviction that so deformed a child could only have been conceived in some specially flagrant infidelity of Ess's while his back was momentarily turned. And, from their vantage point in Swiss Cottage, Vic's mother and father weighed in with dark looks and sighs, knowing in their bones that their son, on whom every care and expense had been lavished, and whose upbringing and education had been a model of progressive enlightenment, had been inveigled into marriage by a neurotic whore.

At the time, Victor and Ess were living in self-imposed penury in Earl's Court. Just as Ess had decided that her daughter must be put in a home, the poor thing contracted pneumonia and died. As Boomer describes them, the details were harrowing. Vic left Ess to cope with the death and burial on her own, going off for a weekend that stretched into a month with a male admirer, in a cottage down among the publishers in Gloucestershire. Boomer, whose view of Victor is surprisingly charitable, took the line that his aesthetic cravings were a manifestation of his shaky sexual identity. That Ess represented his last attempt to achieve normality, and that the distaste he experienced with Ess was transposed into a false impulse towards Beauty. Once this project had failed, he was free to become perfectly commonplace. Boomer's analyses aren't normally that neat. Usually there are more loose ends attached. I'd guess, all the same, that it's more nearly true than false. A marriage hatched in cuckooland. And the moment the thread was broken and love's bubble had burst, Vic became a complete irrelevance in Ess's eyes — as though he'd been an unfortunate episode in someone else's biography.

While Boomer stitched painfully to and fro across the history of his marriage, I remembered Penny telling me that Ess's moment of truth occurred outside Sainsbury's. She'd done her shopping, and as she stood on the pavement, the handle of her bag broke scattering her goods far and wide : the last straw. Rather than plunging after her tins and pats of butter, she just stood there aghast. Aghast at a good deal.

When she came back into focus, it was to see a large unromantic figure of a man — Boomer — casting about on the ground, gathering the packages and tins together into the semblance of a heap. After much fumbling with the half-squashed and half-torn, he squeezed the lot back into her broken shopping basket, and stood before her, with the whole assemblage in his arms.

How it all went from there, I'm not quite sure, but it

went quickly. He escorted her to her flat, and they went to bed together then and there. But although Ess's romantic bubble had burst, both the disentanglement of their previous commitments and their re-entanglement one with the other, took some time.

Boomer was living with sensible Samantha Elston. I hadn't realised that either. In many ways Sam is Ess's obverse: she's the kind of woman who swears forthrightly and knows *everything* about birth control. Boomer says she managed him; but it had been going on for years, and he was bored. She would have bored me too. All her opinions are what you'd wish for, but there's no more to her than what she says or does. It's as if Sam has no access to her own interior life. Boomer called her opaque; and what he fell for in Ess was the opposite of that: a quality of translucency. At first it must have remained a pleasant suspicion; but now, looking back, he spoke as if he'd recognised it instantly, before they'd exchanged a word.

Having a matter-of-fact turn of mind, it probably took Ess some time to realise that Boomer idealised her. And as Boomer rambled on over the circumstances of their courtship, tracking back every now and then to say something more about Vic, it occurred to me that Ess's lack of self-confidence might have had its point of origin in the miseries she'd endured as a child over the colour of her hair.

Only the other day, she and I exchanged school horror stories over supper. She described the small private institution she'd been sent to, where the girls specialised in the refinements of social cruelty. They'd perceived, rightly, that Ess's hair wasn't just ginger, itself a suspect category, but was something altogether more antic. Its sheer luxuriance must have set their nerves on edge. Anyway, they gave her the works. And as a result she grew up convinced that the lustrous fibres sprouting from her scalp were an aberration. From time to time, she conducted experiments with bleaches and dyes, until on one occasion she created a humiliating streak across her crown that nothing would disguise. In despair, she clipped the whole swathe off and explained it to her mother as an accident that had occurred in leaning over a burning candle.

I'd guess that Vic respected it as a stage prop, but that it was not until she met Boomer that she could accept her hair as a legitimate focus of fascination. And this sense of her own peculiarity cut so deep that there was no manoeuvre in the social life of an adult that she felt she could perform without ending in a puddle of ridicule. She was very competent, of course. But it was the competence of someone who has a malign fairy godmother somewhere in the background, ready to wave her wand and banish her — back to the schoolroom with its worn oak desks and oiled parquet floor, trying, somehow, to disguise the biological truth about herself from the little matrons sitting behind her : the blazing efflorescence of her hair.

As we wore ragged, it was Victor that Boomer kept working his way back to ; a topic he'd shut off in some cupboard when he'd first met Ess, but could now bring out to the light of day. What bothered him most was Victor's reaction to the death of his child ; or, more exactly, his own inability to protect Ess from that reaction. Evidently, Vic had excelled himself. He'd threatened to take Ess to court, claiming that his daughter had contracted pneumonia and died through Ess's neglect. Solicitors' letters began to arrive. And with characteristic ineptitude, they circled around grievances that were imaginary, while Vic failed to notice what the simplest inquiry would have told him : that his wife was having an affair with Boomer Mulloy.

In time, the torrent of Victor's spleen abated, and for no apparent reason. I'm not sure whether Ess saw him again, but I rather think he appeared one day, gathered up an armful of belongings, and disappeared. He left behind him, though, some astounding private correspondence ; declarations of devotion and desire from three members of his own sex, one of them in public life and in a position to have learnt more tact.

Anyway, Vic evaporated, leaving behind him the intensest conceivable smell of ordure. It was then the divorce that Boomer wanted to talk about. It had all taken time ; and it was a year at least before anything was essayed. In those far-off days divorce law was based on the principle of the matrimonial offence ; and the only offence that Vic had committed, as far as Ess knew, and as far as Boomer could find out, was that he was unlivable with. This had to be portrayed as mental cruelty.

Ess's performance in the divorce court itself sounds most surprising. According to Boomer, their lawyer spent fully an hour beforehand, trying to coax Ess into an appropriately vivid recital of her woes ; but while he became more and more exasperated, Ess succeeded only in becoming mauve with strain. The case was uncontested, Victor by this time having washed his hands of the marriage and everything connected with it. It was a contest not against his lawyers, but against the scepticism of the judge, appointed by society to prevent divorce by consent. Physical cruelty, black eyes and contusions, such men understand, but mental cruelty is a category they were bound to view with suspicion. Anyway, the case was called with Ess still tongue-tied. Her lawyer must have been steeling himself for a débâcle : a case thrown out and his reputation dented.

Ess sat there frozen. But when the moment came, she was transformed. She described Victor's antics with clarity : his departure to Gloucestershire as the child was dying, his jealous rages and head-bangings. She did not recriminate ; but she left no room for doubt. She told the truth with a conviction that rarely graces it ; and for ten minutes or so, made it unchallengeable. The judge was bowled over. He granted the decree nisi without a quibble, and could he have done so with propriety would doubtless have asked her out to supper too. In Boomer's eyes, Ess was for those moments wholly transparent ; a theatrical feat of the highest flight.

In flashes, then, intermittently, Ess had an impressive gift for self-representation. It was one that she'd deploy in crises ; but from time to time to keep her hand in too. Dropping in for Saturday lunch, I've seen her transform herself from the cool and preoccupied Ess awaiting Boomer's return from work, into a seductress unwrapping for him an elaborate confection of misrepresentation about what he was going to get for his birthday. She was teasing him ; but flattering him at the same time, showing him that he was worth the effort. Boomer was pleased and slightly rattled. It was only a feint. But there were others, and they could disconcert.

Having trampled that pasture, Boomer's anxiety carried him further afield, looping out beyond Ess and Victor, to encompass other facets of his dissatisfaction with himself. My attention kept slipping back to the mortuary. Edging back into the flow after one of these sorties, I found Boomer struggling with yet another of his bemusements – an office crisis in which husbands and wives, lovers and loved, had moved around him in arcs that he could make no sense of. An innocent abroad, not in the know. His only points of anchorage had been in his work and in sexual intercourse with Ess. Ess whom he idealised, but now must do without.

By two in the morning, I'd administered sleeping pills; and once Boomer was out of the way, found myself carried from one eddy of disaster's backwash to another. The curiosity about Ess that had buoyed me up disappeared, and in its place the desolation of wasted lives and mutilation. Sometimes as driver, sometimes as passenger, I relived Perce and Ess's crash – a night I'm grateful to have survived.

When I first met Ess, I imagined a background obscurely formidable: a dad who was a professor of classics somewhere out in the sticks, say, or a county court judge. But when I met him at the wedding party, Dad stood revealed as a mild-mannered dentist from Harrogate who did conjuring tricks for children in his spare time.

What we talked about was Ess's cat. Ess had been an only child, and her mother had played a great deal of bridge. The while, Ess communed with a huge ginger tom called Leighton. When piano practice became a serious part of her life, she arranged Leighton's bedding beside her so that he would keep her company while she played. He died when Ess was in her impressionable teens; and she flung herself into her music in earnest, practising not to stave off boredom or loneliness, but for the gratification it can provide. 'Such a passionate nature,' he'd said.

'So unlike her mother,' he'd added, with carefully

poised disloyalty. And so unlike you too, I'd silently rejoined.

The image of young Ess's superlative head set side by side with the more moth-eaten ginger of a bad old tom is a comforting one to dwell on. Why 'Leighton'? The explanation was prosaic. He'd come from an aunt in Leighton Buzzard, married to a chief librarian. Ess's dad looks up to this brother-in-law of his; and Ess must have learnt of Leighton Buzzard as a spot where traces of charisma were to be found, qualities of which her tom became the living embodiment. He'd started out in life as 'Orlando', but then became 'Orlando Leighton', and soon enough just 'Leighton'. Ess's father was punctilious in his concern that I should grasp all this.

I hardly spoke to Ess's Ma, but she fits to a tee the role of a bridge player — rather a good bridge player — married to a Harrogate dentist. But in hindsight, I think I detect a certain romantic potentiality that her dentist had missed. As though she'd taken refuge in bridge from some private disappointment or failure of nerve. Like her daughter perhaps, she'd hidden from anguish in skill. And like her, she looks as though such externally acquired finesse could be harnessed, if occasion arose, to purposes that were altogether more intimate. They were rather alike physically, too: the hair, though the mother's was faded, and also the skin — large freckles and violet shadows, the sort of complexion that blisters wickedly in the sun, but never tans. Mother and daughter: two women in whom the light of a cool and accurate sensuality flickered, but never quite shone? Or an unmarried imagination running away with itself? It's so hard to tell.

When he surfaced, Boomer looked more haggard than ever, and immediately settled on a course of checking up.

He needed to make sure that their empty house was all right. He needed to make a statement to the relevant police officers. He needed to establish details about post mortem and inquest. He needed to tell Ess's parents, and arrange to see them. He needed to see what was left of Perce's car. He needed to inspect the scene of the accident. He needed to get in touch with Penny, which I suggested was not timely. And he needed to identify Ess. His impulse was to do this at once, before breakfast, beginning with a visit to their house to pick up the family Peugeot. This I absolutely forbade, forcing him to sit down and ingest some breakfast cereal and milky coffee; and then give me an undertaking that he would drive nowhere under his own steam, one accident being ample.

But delay though I could, Boomer was compelled to complete his circuit, so we made the mournful round. The mortuary, I could not bring myself to enter for a second time. When he got back into the car, Boomer was trembling, pathetically scrubbing his hands one against the other. And when we reached the scene of the accident itself, we were both too distracted to do more than stare. The road snakes there along the spine of a narrow ridge, woodland falling away on one side. The tree when we found it was its unmistakable self: a silver birch tilting half out of the ground. Leading up to it, on to the soft shoulder (another wonderful title, incidentally), a path of skid-marks and churned earth. The tree, the earth, the skid-marks all seemed quite devoid of information. Likewise Perce's Jaguar in the police yard. It stood in line, beyond a caved-in BMC Maxi and a half-crushed Triumph Spitfire. The Jaguar was a write-off; but considering two people died inside it, wasn't as severely damaged as I would have expected. As we stood, I wondered whether Boomer's compulsion for the full story, for every pertinent detail, was going to force him to look inside. But discretion won, and he contented himself with walking round to the front of the car, and peering at the inside from a distance of nine or ten feet. He hesitated, looked as though he was going to confront what there was not the least point in confronting, and then, at last, came away.

As we made our way out of that politely rural district and headed back to Town, we touched for the first time on the raw nerve at the centre of this hateful business. What the hell were Perce and Ess doing there together in the first place?

My account of the matter to the police had been that Ess and Perce were old family friends; that the Mulloys and the Coburns were a happy foursome. Mrs Mulloy and Mr Coburn were of irreproachable moral character; and there was nothing more natural in the world than that, their spouses being away, they should take an evening spin together in the country. But if it had been an evening spin, it was a damned long one: they were forty miles from home when they crashed, and they were heading north, suggesting that they had been even further afield.

A spin in the country would do for the police, and it will do for the coroner; but it'll scarcely wash among ourselves. And why precisely had they gone off the road? Perce rarely drank more than a pint, and drove with what he considered panache, but which the rest of us perceived as decent care. 'Perhaps he had a stroke ... ?' Boomer's query struck an unpleasant note of ambiguity as it trailed away. (There's a Simenon in which a nightmarish accident with a school bus is caused by a driver stroking his mistress's thigh.) Perhaps Perce had swerved to avoid an oncoming car, and the driver had been too scared or drunk to stop. Even more likely, they'd swerved to avoid a straying deer — we'd seen warning signs not a hundred yards from where their car had come to rest. But Perce's attention could have been distracted. Was it conceivable that they were having a clandestine affair?

I took refuge behind the possible implications of the 'Beware Deer' signs, and for the time being Boomer was as relieved as I was to sheer away from the accident's more grotesque implications. There are moments when even the tidiest mind boggles, and it's usually best to let it have its way.

Reaching home, I judged it time I saw Penny; but was keen to see her on my own, without Boomer, so that I could draw whatever sting she might hold in store for him. I love my sister, but wariness was justified. For the time being she's a dangerous companion.

We kissed, as we always kiss. On the point of letting me go, she turned back, kissed me again, this time on the mouth, and then clung to me, crying, but without making a sound. Patting her on the back, I felt I had misjudged her. Possibly, after all, she was going to express her grief without trying to mangle someone else in the process. And as it happens I *had* misjudged her, taking an altogether too melodramatic view of what such mangling is going to consist of.

We stood for five minutes or so. She rubbed the side of her face against mine, and the tears spread all over both our cheeks. I began to choke, too, with nostalgia for the years we spent together while we were still young. Kissing me again with an absent-minded abandonment about her mouth suggesting that she'd confused me with one of her lovers, she pulled herself together, and led me by the hand to sit opposite her. Our chairs were so close that she could hold my hands, and press her knees against my own. It was a while before she spoke, but when she did, it was blunt:

'Very sly. She must have needed a screw.'

Lulled by tears, but sharpened by years of surprise attacks and booby-trapping, I had just enough wit left to point out that we'd no evidence either way, and that she was bound to be guessing. Unconvinced, she was watching my face with care. In the end, she heaved herself up and sat herself on my lap, holding my face against her breast. A gesture of primitive nurture. It was her turn to pat my head, to comfort me. Between twins, physical intimacy is sometimes quite close to the intimacy that exists between the divided elements of a single mind. It's claim is quite direct, and stripped of all fascination. Add to this the curious sense of dissociation that many actresses seem to have about their own bodies, and hers was temporarily an entity over which she exercised no proprietorial right at all.

'Sly, even if I can't prove it.'

And then, after a long pause:

'How long's it been going on d'you think?' She was serving notice that she was going to take an altogether earthier view of Ess's motives than I had. Perhaps any woman would have done the same. Even Ess herself.

May 15th

In recollection, the inquest hovers like a bilious hallucination. What actually happened and what felt as though it was about to happen, I cannot now disentangle. I can't recall an occasion on which what people said has been so swamped in recollection by what they might have said. A second Simenon vignette — the literal devoured by the literary.

Boomer and Penny were there, and I went too, hoping to provide moral support. Penny was kind to Boomer, hugging him, and holding his hand. In as much as she's intent on dismantling his ego, she's decided to postpone the operation till later. The while, he was glancing around, drumming his fingers, rubbing his hands. His intelligence was still clicking, but he was running ragged, and looked as though he might flare up at some quite trivial provocation.

The coroner proved a silken gentleman, with convoluted games to play : blonde hair scrupulously parted, and pale blue eyes gazing at us through rimless spectacles. His stock in trade is probing around in the sensibilities of the bereaved. Too subtle to be interested in causing pain forthrightly, he's fascinated with his own skill in fingering relatives' sense of shame. A bully would have glanced at the story of an evening spin shared by family friends of irreproachable moral character and reached at once for post-mortem evidence to show that the two deceased had recently had sexual intercourse. A gentler spirit would have gone through the motions of accepting the story at its face value ; would express his solemn regret ; and would do his best to ensure that no incriminating evidence reached the relatives' ears. Our man fished with more skill. He offered his regrets at this sad affair, and floated the odd phrase before us about lives cut off in their prime. But the while he was eyeing Boomer, to see how much provocation he would stand without sparking an outright confrontation. Consultant engineers are not creatures he meets every day, and might react unexpectedly. He looked to me like a man with a poor third-class degree tucked away somewhere in his *curriculum vitae*: a point of perceived inferiority that would make Boomer a tempting but dangerous bait. He was also eyeing Penny, I think misreading her as a successful businessman's plump and appealing moll.

He moved forward softly, with an unpleasant fastidiousness, through 'these regrettably necessary formalities', sensitive to the least inkling of how formidable his two victims were, and where their points of self-doubt might lie. He was wise to be cautious. Boomer can erupt, and Penny you underestimate at your peril. They made a curious trio: this crimped country solicitor, looking for shreds of sentiment that he could play with; and, in their different ways, Boomer and Penny on guard.

'It's my painful duty ... ' Et cetera, et cetera. He was moving into a consideration of the immediate causes of the accident, his legitimate concern. 'Was he to understand ... ?' Yes, he was to understand that there was no other vehicle involved. 'Could he take it ... ?' Yes, he could take it that the police had checked, and that there was no evidence of another car having braked sharply or swerved, before making off in the opposite direction. 'Might he be reminded ... ?' Yes, he could be reminded that, in the last five years, there had been no less than twelve accidents in this district in which deer or other animals had strayed on to the road, and in three of these fatalities had resulted. 'As far as he could recall ... ' Yes, indeed, this *was* an area of the forest where deer had frequently been seen to stray on to the road, and where there was no fencing to prevent this. 'Most regrettable, most regrettable.'

Still with his eye on Boomer and on Penny, he then moved to the question of other contributing circumstances. The post-mortem evidence — another glance at Penny — made it abundantly plain that Mr Coburn had had very little to drink that evening : a single whisky perhaps. Mrs Mulloy, the report indicated — a longish lingering glance at Boomer — had had considerably more than that to drink, the equivalent, say, of four whiskies. But this was immaterial because there was no question but that it was Mr Coburn who had been driving, not Mrs Mulloy. I watched Boomer with some nervousness, to see whether the coroner was having any success. Was his literal mind dwelling as mine was, on the violence that had been done to Ess's body to ascertain this : incisions made by some ape with a sharp knife. Or had he risen to the more succulent part of the coroner's bait? If so, he would by now be worrying why Ess should have been drinking so much more than he would have expected. And so much more than Perce, who had presumably been quaffing judicious tomato juices, while she downed her gins and tonic with a gesture that I knew well. He looked frightful, but remained staring down at his hands, listening. I wondered how our man was going to edge on to trickier topics still, but didn't have long to wait. 'The statements before him made it plain ... ' Made it plain that Mrs Mulloy and Mr Coburn were old family friends of long standing ; that, indeed, the two couples were on the friendliest terms. 'The bereaved would forgive him if he asked ... ' Asked for confirmation that this was so, because he was constrained by the duties of his post to discover if there was any extraneous circumstance or pressure that might explain this lamentable accident. Did those who had made statements wish in any respect to

49

elaborate upon what they had already said : a lingering look around all three of us. 'No ... ?' A long, carefully judged pause. Then he must also be reminded that there was no further evidence that might suggest an undue strain between Mr Coburn and Mrs Mulloy — another glance at Boomer to see how he was taking it — evidence he hastened to say that was pertinent only in as much as it might contribute to a lapse of the driver's attention. 'No ... ?' And then, placing his words with puss-foot care, he reassured himself that there was no other evidence to suggest a degree of intimacy between the deceased that went beyond that of good friends. 'No, of *course* there was not ...'

Boomer was now frozen still, his mind, I'd not the slightest doubt, torturing itself with a visualisation of how that set of routine checks had been performed.

Penny muttered 'dirty bastard' under her breath beside me. My anxiety switched at once to her and the risk that she was about to make a richly deserved intervention ; one that the coroner would take with him to his grave. But he was as sensitive to this new threat as he had been, a moment earlier, to the possibility of provoking Boomer, and he immediately backed down, drawing our part of the proceedings to a close, introducing a catch, even a falter, into his presentation to show that his sympathy with Mrs Coburn in her loss was from the heart, sincere.

My fevered imagination may well have supplied some of the detail. Looking back, it seems unlikely that any coroner would allow so much of his Id to show. But wrapped in his robe he lingers as an insect that takes its chances, and sups well, leaving behind its visiting card — those few droplets of alien protein that'll wreak their havoc as the days go by. A lucky man to find a job in which his needs were so neatly catered for. He can toy with danger : the chance that an enraged and unexpectedly sharp-tongued victim will pollute the measured calm of his court. And at the same time, he can relish both his legitimacy and his skill. He'll never become grand : a judge. He's not tough enough. But he's found his niche, and fills it to a tee.

May 16th

On our way home from the inquest, we stopped for a meal that none of us could eat. Penny in particular was silent. Through my head like a maddening tune went a name : 'Otis Sistrunk'. In fancy, the mortician who keeps spare parts at home with him in the ice box. In fact, defensive tackle for the Oakland Raiders.

I caught myself posing thoughtful questions on the nature of violence to my private seminar. Is the behemoth who weighs 255 pounds and works in a meat-packing factory any more violent than the mouse who dreams of being 255 pounds and a behemoth? It was a rousing session and the girls loved it ; but it didn't bring back Ess.

This evening, Boomer confessed that he was being plagued too : by rhymes. Samantha had once shown him a poem that started 'Rat you call, and rat I come ... ' And Boomer's head is now full of schemes in which thumb, plum, hum, dumb, bum, chum, slum, crumb play their parts. I hadn't thought of Sam as a versifier. Apparently it's something she did only when unhappy. I asked whether she'd been on his mind, but he said not in the least. It just wasn't that kind of a relationship. To his best knowledge, these were its only echoes.

May 17th

A day in Bonn, and a moratorium on my woes. The sobriety of German civil servants releases in me a cheerfully clubbable self I would not normally have known was there.

May 23rd

A day that became five days. Now I'm back, Perce is underground in his elm box, and Ess a plume of smoke that's mingled with the traffic fumes and gone. Boomer left a note in erratic handwriting to say that he's gone home to sort things out. I've rung Penny and she sounds more poised. Of the funerals, all she'd say was that I was lucky to have missed them both. She'll be moving back home at the end of the week. The girls are back at school, and she wants to clear the decks. Penny and Boomer, only a few doors apart, each sorting through the remnants of their marriages. As plain as the hand before me, they're fated to form some sort of relationship. The only questions are when, and what sort it'll be.

May 29th

A chance to chat to Boomer. He looks as though he's lost a couple of stone in weight; his collar's loose, and his suit's baggy around him. He's still in the grip of his zeal for arrangements, but the number he can make is now running out. Soon he'll have to untie knots in order to have ends to re-tie.

He's not a man for locker-room confidences, but he can be forthright. Over our scampi and chips, he announced that mad thoughts were circling inside his head. For the first time, he wonders whether he might not be paranoid. I tried to deflect him but couldn't; so instead set about persuading him that paranoia is a rational response to the outrage devised by others behind our backs. Unexpectedly, I struck a chord; with Boomer, you never know. Some wretch in his head office has just laid waste to one of Boomer's protégés; and Boomer's convinced the attack was triggered by what's happened to Ess. Instead of commiserating with Boomer, however briefly, this functionary has held back, embarrassed, and then taken a swipe at someone whom he knows Boomer wants to protect. And when Boomer expostulates, he backs down, implying (but not quite saying) that if Mr Mulloy is going to play on everyone's feelings, there's nothing for him to say.

I told him about the Isbisters, and what happened when their son was killed by a car. Bertie had just published his first book, and one of the great men of his own university chose to savage it. Some of the Isbisters' friends shied away too. Or attacked them. I quoted Bertie's Law which holds that the quickest way to shed your intellectual friends is to lose a child in an accident. The only people who could show them affection — who were not disablingly embarrassed — were people who had no interest whatever in the life of the mind.

None of this did much, though, to quiet the creatures creeping up and down Boomer's spine. He hummed, harred and looked uncomfortable, spilling his sugar on the carpet; but all he'd commit himself to was a rambling disquisition on rugby football.

There were two strands, one moral and the other more spiritual. Had I been at the Varsity match towards the end of the forties, when Kininmonth had picked off the Cambridge winger in full flight? As it happens, I had : a moment to cherish for a lifetime. But for Boomer, a moment heavy with implications I had not noticed. Perhaps it's still true ; I don't know. But in those days, Boomer told me, the number 8 was supposed to lift his head from each scrum, and if the enemy had won the ball, trudge off in the direction of his own corner flag, offering himself as a last line of defence. A thankless task, because if the action came his way, he almost always arrived too late.

That day, Oxford had Cambridge trapped inside their own twenty-five, but lost the ball. Smoothly it went down the Cambridge line ; their winger, too fast, rounded the defence, and set off down the length of the Twickenham turf towards the Oxford line. He sped like a pellet, and, already an Oxford supporter, I watched in horrified fascination. Out of space, there then emerged the angular figure of Kininmonth, the Oxford number 8, corner-flagging for Christ and all that's decent. The paths of the dark blue and pale blue figures intersected, and with a yard or two to spare, Kininmonth scythed that predator down.

It was a triumphant affirmation of duty in the service of the long shot. Boomer was impressed by the scene's ethical underlay. But it also meant something to him more personally, and he told me all about it.

At school, large and clumsy, he'd played in the front row and so was the last person to get up from each scrum. But being last, was also first — the first, that is, to get free from any ensuing ruck or maul. No one knew about 'second phase' in those days, but Boomer set himself the duty of corner flagging from the ruck following the scrum. He always corner flagged, and he always got there too late.

But doggedly he stuck to precept. And one day in the rain he got there after all. The school's pitch had turned to a dish of slime. His own side scored early, but gradually the visitors got the upper hand, and camped, Passchendaele-style, on Boomer's line. The enemy had a battle-cruiser of a wing-threequarter, nasty tempered ; and before too long he'd scored, giving one of Boomer's team-mates as he did so a meaty and illegal punch in the eye.

For a while, Boomer's side clung desperately to their draw. But there was another scrum, another ruck. Both were lost, and, for the second time, that winger raised steam and set sail for the line. He had twenty yards in which to build up momentum, and could not have deviated even had he wished to. Boomer held him in his sights the whole way in, his fear of violence overcome by the attractions of revenge. They met within a yard of the corner, and Boomer bundled him Rugby League-style into touch, uprooting the corner flag, and banging *Scharnhorst*'s head on a sodden duck-board.

The line was saved, the match was saved, and you would think that despite it's *Boys' Own* echoes, it would be a memory to cherish. But not so. There should have been a percussive impact, and this did not occur. The battle-cruiser turned out to be fleshy, and even the blow of head on duck-board was glancing. A golden opportunity had been missed : for once, Boomer had been in a position to utter a deep-felt need by means of a physical act, and he'd blurred eloquence's edges, played safe. A violent and comprehensive bundling had taken place, but there had been no definitively cleansing bang.

On the face of it, the story of a grieving man who wishes he were free to lash out. But as he told it, the story of a man who has lived with a woman he idealised, and now knows that he has lost the opportunity to utter himself to her without reservation.

I tried to say something comforting about there always being regret; and that eloquence — physical or verbal — is never quite what it seems. Either we play safe and despise ourselves; or commit ourselves neck and crop, and then are left to cope with our own shock or guilt. But Boomer was in no mood to be consoled, and wandered off on to another tack altogether: graveyard wit. Finally, 'dead right' was all I could find to say: an unusual turn of phrase, when you come to think of it. But while some unintentional puns are worth exploring, others are best left alone. 'Dead right' seemed to me to fall squarely into the second category.

May 31st

Today I'd spent an hour fishing for a story-line in the midst of some word-blind incompetent's first draft, and had begun to build anew, buttressing at the appropriate moments with facts and figures, when I caught myself doodling in the margin about Ess and Perce. These doodles turned into a spectrum of rival interpretations of their outing together, ranging from the flagrantly culpable to innocent.

Most culpable and obvious: they were having an affair. And the dislocation Boomer kept hinting at could have been either effect or cause. He could have felt uneasy because, unknown to him, his wife was carrying on with her best friend's spouse. Alternatively, she could have been driven to look further afield (and by any standard, Perce was a lot further), because her marriage turned on a fatally placed flaw. But although there's no evidence beyond its inherent absurdity that rules it out decisively, a well-established love-affair strikes me as unlikely. They would have had to be away from home concurrently, and Penny would have been bound to notice.

A shade less comprehensively culpable: what about a casual tumble? A spring impulse. Sex that Ess sought to reassure herself that although she was forty, life still held hope; and sex that Perce was only too willing to provide. What you can't imagine, you can't be expected to perceive. True. But I'd seen not a shadow nor flicker of it.

Or perhaps a bond that was secret but platonic? Ess could have been moved by pity for Perce; or — just conceivably — by jealousy or distrust of Penny. While for Perce, secrecy would have been its own reward.

Or something quite blameless? Perce finds that the weather is beautiful and that Penny is away, so he rings the Mulloys, discovers Ess at a loose end, and, without more ado, they agree on an evening spin. Nothing more, nothing less.

What are the clues? Ess had been drinking quite hard, while Perce hadn't: a sign, perhaps, of depression to be overcome. Or of nerves to be steeled for intimacies later. As I understand the coroner's glance towards the evidence from the post mortem, they had not had intercourse. But that proves nothing. They might have had no intention of going to bed together. Or they could have been relishing the prospect, but saving it until later. One of them might have had carnal intent but not the other. Perce but not

57

Ess. Or vice versa. As usual, the facts tell you little unless you already know the underlying motive. For all I know, Boomer and Ess had had a major row or estrangement that they managed to cover up. I could ask Penny.

June 1st

'Christ knows' was all I got for my pains. For a moment, I thought she was going to follow this up with the proposal that we mind our own business. The thought was in the air, but in the end it was not formulated in so many words. Although she's secretive about her own comings and goings, I'd expected her to be candid about Ess.

I also asked Penny whether she'd seen much of Boomer, but again got nothing. She'd popped round once or twice to see that he was all right, and why was I interested to know? She did volunteer that he was coming round for a meal, but not in a tone to suggest that we could enter into a collusive discussion of his welfare. I can never tell in advance whether her moods of brusqueness are negotiable or not. You have to risk a rebuttal that stings. I chose to leave well alone.

June 4th

This morning Penny rang me at the office, in itself a rarity. An undisclosed 'something' has come from the police. I tried to get her to tell me what it was, but she couldn't talk about it on the phone. I had got to go down, and how soon could I be there? Why not straight away?

I'd been called out of a meeting of some delicacy to take her call and told her so ; but transacted the rest of my business with a laughable lack of concentration, being visited by all sorts of horror from poisoned pen letters to severed limbs.

When I got there, just before supper, the girls were home, and it was Sue who let me in, warning me, as if I needed any warning, that her Ma was in a bate. She hugged me enthusiastically — enthusiastically, that is, taking her low baseline level of activity into account — and I enjoyed the seemly pleasure of rubbing my hands up and down the sides of her lower rib cage, noticing as I did so that she'd grown a little thin. Uncles, I've discovered, exist to provide their nieces with practice.

The rings under her eyes are darker, and her hair needs a shampoo ; but her father's demise seems to have marked Sue only slightly. In tacit protest against their mother's excesses, they're conventional ; but this conventionality never amounted to a vote in favour of their Dad. Rather, an abstention. One's always known this. Their religious tendencies probably have the same root. Sue's over hers now, but Jane's still ensnared. Sue's muttered report on the deployment of the household confirmed this : 'Ma's in bed. Janey's out praying.'

Like Penny a few days ago, she was on the point of leading me into the sitting room when she turned back and hugged me again. I half expected her to cry too, and rub her tears into my face with her cheek ; but she just hugged me that second time, and wended her distant way ahead of me among Penny's unsatisfactory sofas and chairs. Unlike her mother, she sat apart, and the look she directed was towards the window. After some time, she observed that her mother had taken it quite well, all things considered, but that it wasn't as if they'd been happy like Ess and Boomer. I asked about Boomer's visit to supper; and it was divulged only that she and Jane had done the cooking — a soufflé — and that it had flopped.

I asked what was upsetting Penny, but all I learnt was that it was a parcel. Her habitually sceptical tone, though, brought my fantasies back to earth, and thoughts of bloodied torsos wrapped in sacking receded. In all probability, it was a bundle of bits and pieces from the Jaguar that'd been tucked away in dashboard or boot.

If Sue had had the sophistication her mother wished for, she would have offered me a drink; but instead she stared out of the window, where there was another memorable sunset in the making, and left me to forage for myself. She fiddled for a while with something that had gone wrong with her shoe, then suggested I go up and see Penny. Not bossily, just giving her point of view. I enjoy the sense of distance that she creates so effortlessly around her. A social space into which you can wander without fear of fire-crackers. Or machine-gun fire. Around Penny, there's a sense of distance too, but it's crawling with danger. Only an ardent suicide would enter it blindfold.

It is part of Penny's power that she is never quite in the state of mind I expect. By the time I got to her bedroom, she was over the worst, and apologising for being such a silly cow.

Following her glance, I saw two holdalls perched on her dresser, trussed up with a good deal of constabulary string. Dumping them on the bed between us, I realised why she'd been queasy. Lying there side by side, they were the last remains of two people's intentions: the bundled up remnants of two systems of hope.

Why had they both come to Penny? The answer to that was simple. His holdall was labelled. *Everything* of Perce's was labelled. But Ess's bore no identifying sign. It was hers all the same: from Prisunic. She'd shown it to us as part of her holiday loot. Recognising them was one thing, though; opening them another. In the first place there was the question of legality: of whether we'd a right to open Ess's bag, or ought to pass it unopened to Boomer. I was concerned that Boomer's feelings should not be lacerated gratuitously; but aware, too, that whatever the state of his sensibilities, he needed to know every detail.

Penny said nothing, but was clearly doing ethical sums of her own. In the end, after five minutes or so, in which I paced around Penny's room, and neither of us said a word, she achieved the resolution she needed. Without more ado, I was instructed to 'open the bloody things'; and when I showed signs of anxiety, she said that we could throw away anything incriminating before Boomer saw it. She spoke with an assumed authority for him that took me by surprise. So I did as I was bid, the only concession to the ambiguities of my role being my decision to begin with Perce's holdall, not Ess's.

Dead men's luggage you touch with some temerity. It's almost easier to touch their bodies. All signs of sentience depart from a corpse, whereas in luggage they can linger. Perce's proved mercifully impersonal. There was nothing in it to twist your sympathies around in ways for which you are unprepared. But there could be not the slightest doubt: it was a bag packed for an overnight stay. Pyjamas, towel, change of underclothes and shirt, sponge bag, electric razor in its case. Also, incongruously, a file; and in it some business correspondence with a light engineering firm in Crawley New Town. Uppermost was a letter

61

from a Mr Fredericks saying that he was looking forward to meeting Mr Coburn at 2.30 on the afternoon of the crash. Upending the holdall, I also discovered an Ambler paperback. And, the only detail to touch a nerve, a squash ball that Perce must in a lapse from tidiness have failed to remove the last time he'd played.

I held up the sponge bag to Penny and she nodded her approval. Opening it, I emptied the contents on to the bedspread. A nail file. A toothbrush, badly worn ; for a neat man, excessively worn. A small plastic bottle of sleeping tablets. A small tube of toothpaste, squeezed unsystematically — again out of character. A small bottle of after-shave lotion. A pre-wrapped cake of soap. A flannel with 'P' embroidered in the corner. And a white envelope. And in that envelope a packet of condoms. Unopened.

Penny and I stared at each other, while I sat foolishly holding up the offending packet between finger and thumb. I was trying to think of something to say, and Penny started to cry. Poor bloody Perce, she said, he never did have any sense of style.

While Penny continued to stare at the wall, red-eyed, I set about Ess's bag, already regretting our decision to pry. The first item was a freshly laundered white cotton nightie : Laura Ashley, unless I'm mistaken. She would have looked stunningly severe in it, an aesthetic *coup* as lost on Perce as any could be. Next a sweater and scarf. A pair of slippers. A library book : Jean Rhys's *Good Morning Midnight*. And a sponge bag. Again I held it up, and again she nodded ; then reached over and took it from me, emptying it herself. Out fell some items of make-up. A toothbrush. Toothpaste. A flannel. A tube of antihistamine cream. A nail file. A small pair of scissors. A wad of face tissues. And that was all.

I attempted a jocularity about there at least being no Conovid, but it fell flat. Penny looked through me as though I were a speck on a window pane. Then, explaining the commonplace to a half-wit, told me that Ess had had her tubes tied, so contraception was for her an irrelevance. I hadn't known this; but nor evidently had Perce. Otherwise, he wouldn't have been sporting those distressing sheaths. It follows that they could not have been to bed together; and that this was their very first time.

Penny sobbed and I wandered. Why should a disciminating woman like Ess pick on Perce? If she had had an urge to diversify, why hadn't she chosen an affectionate bachelor like me? Others had, why not her? And what were the two of us going to say to Boomer? Whatever their precise implication, those two items of evidence — Ess's nightie and Perce's condoms — are going to be hard to reconcile with Boomer's somewhat idealised view of Ess's character, or for that matter my own. Penny's view, the earthier one, is gathering weight.

Half-heartedly, I tried to air my uneasinesses, but Penny cut me short. With the same assumed authority, she told me I had more important things to worry about, and if asked to plead ignorance. I wanted to know what she was going to say, but she brushed this aside; and still red-eyed but more cheerful, she led me back downstairs.

June 5th

This morning, between calls, I gave Friend Fredericks a ring. Yes, Mr Coburn had called as arranged. They'd had a mutually advantageous chat, and Mr Coburn had left after an hour, saying that he was going to make use of a beautiful day and drive on down to the sea.

Was anyone with him? Not to his knowledge. And had he been at all specific about his route? Fredericks had understood Perce to mean that he was heading down the motorway to Brighton. But he couldn't be sure, so it's now a matter for guesswork. I do know though that Perce favoured a *Good Food Guide* pub just behind the Downs in Steyning, so on the off-chance I gave them a ring too. Mr Coburn had booked a single room for that night, but had cancelled at the last moment. How late in the day? That same morning, the girl thought.

In other words, I've been unintelligent but lucky. He sometimes went there with Penny, so wouldn't go there with Ess. If I'd used my wits, I wouldn't have rung; but if I'd used my wits, I wouldn't have learnt that Perce had changed his plans at the last moment. The possibility of a long-standing affair between them is ruled out more or less conclusively by poor Perce's packet of condoms. And this last-minute rearrangement makes the whole thing look more like a festive caper. Between them, however, those self-same condoms and Ess's nightie preclude, or almost preclude, a totally innocent venture. Just conceivably, Perce popped that envelope into his bag on the off-chance. And while Ess manifestly had in mind a night away from home, she could have stipulated separate bedrooms, and an embargo on any amorous traffic between them. So the venture could have been platonic on her part, if not on his.

Wishful thinking perhaps, but I can't help feeling that those two books dropped into their respective holdalls are mute testimony, too. Do you pop an Eric Ambler into your bag if you know that a night of carnal exercise is in store? Or for that matter a Jean Rhys? More, they

64

seem like bedside reading with which to while away the minutes before sleep takes hold.

Perce could well have followed a policy of being prepared : for success and for comparative failure too. But Ess ? In hindsight, her choice of text was ominous, to say the least. Her bookmark suggested that she was half-way through ; so she may not have known what Rhys had in store for her. If I remember aright, the heroine gives herself on the last page to the loathesome *maquereau* who's lurked all along. In a seedy hotel bedroom, what's more. It's one of the grimmest denouements in my recollection.

Even if she didn't know where it was leading her, Ess would scarcely have taken so gloomy a tale with her if, even with a tenth part of her imaginative powers, she had an erotic adventure in view. This unlikelihood opens on to others. If both were equipped for a night away, why, at nine o'clock in the evening, were they heading north, away from the sea, rather than towards it ?

A new scenario takes shape. Ess rang Penny, forgetting that she was off at a poetry-reading. Perce answered ; and she told him that Boomer was away and that she was fed up. Perce had to drive down to Crawley the next day, so what about their making a day of it ? Come to that, they could stay the night somewhere. Perce hastily cancelled his booking at the pub, and cast round for an acceptable hotel where he wasn't known. Ess might well have had the day off — a point I can check — and thought why not. Then, at some point in the outing, she discovers that Perce is working his way round to an infidelity. She then falls to downing gin and tonics — either as Dutch courage, or to steel herself to say no. Perhaps there was an altercation of sorts. Anyway, they change their plan, and decide to head back home after all.

As a story it makes sense. I like its general tenor. On the other hand, it doesn't tell you what you really need to know: Ess's state of mind. Her doubts and fears. Whether she could really have been excited at the prospect of going to bed with Perce.

In search of more loose ends, I rang Ess's Bureau. While I was waiting, I flicked over the pages of the *Good Food Guide*, and, as I did so, another unwelcome thought struck me. Far from making their way home, Perce and Ess might have been heading for a *Good Food Guide* hotel that Perce had noted down as lying en route for home. I was leafing through the entries marked on the guide's map, to see whether any might have struck the right note to the rummaging Perce, when Lois Bamford came on the line. For the next ten minutes, my mutually commiserative chat with her was cross-cut with specifications from the guide about the admissibility of invalid carriages, children and dogs, and archly academic characterisations of the establishments' food and drink.

Through the welter of scrambled information reaching my senses, I divined that the tie between Lois and Ess had been closer than I'd realised. She'd been to the cremation, and commented on how lost Boomer had seemed. Curiosity getting the better of me, I suggested a meal out. From the alacrity with which she agreed, and the closeness of the date we've fixed on, I'd guess she's suffering pangs of curiosity too.

June 8th

Lunch with the formidable Lois. Albani's was her idea not mine. Nostalgic it may be, but the food's grim. Half-way

66

through a limp antipasto, I set my inquiries in motion, but learnt little and revealed a good deal. Looking back, I'm bound to admire her negotiative finesse. We began as we were to proceed. I asked whether Ess was at the Bureau on the morning of the day she died. She replied obliquely : we should form a club of Ess's devotees and call ourselves the 'Essenes'. A life on the fringes of big business scarcely primes a man to cope with that sort of bitchy Girtonian erudition ; but prodded sharply enough, I can sometimes reply in kind, without thinking. I reminded her that although the Essenes renounced marriage and shared their worldly goods, they were ascetic ; and as far as Ess was concerned, that scarcely filled the bill.

'And died by throwing themselves from a high place rather than submit to capture ; the last of their line ... ' It was a deft touch, committing us to deep water before I'd felt my way. For a second, her tailored suit and smile struck me as quite exceptionally offensive. A declaration of her own interstitial position in the spectrum of appetites ; and a broad hint, too, that she'd enjoyed an intimacy of access to Ess that mere males could not expect to share.

With more smiles, she relented, but made it plain that she was operating from a position of strength. Ess had been at work, but it was her half-day. As Lois portrayed her, you would hardly have known that she was married, let alone that she might be conducting an affair. Obliging with these snippets, Lois stared at me with eyes that began to look like saucers, quite unblinking. We were in the same boat together ; but she was the coxswain and I was pulling an oar. What the boat is, precisely, I'm still not sure ; but the air of complicity she creates is strong. Almost a polite prurience.

Ess told me once that she liked the Bureau because she never felt forced there to talk about babies or operations. I repeated this, and the word 'operations' seemed to throw a delicately poised switch in Lois's private circuitry. Excited, she started to pump me about the precise causes of death, a terrain over which I'm not prepared to scramble. I told her they'd both been killed outright, a proposition that has approximately the same status, as far as its veracity goes, as the fiction about an evening's spin in the country. Enough was said at the inquest to make it plain that the truth was more harrowing.

Even in fobbing her off, I've the impression that I was feeding Lois gobbets of information that she found gratifying. Just before we parted, she let fall that once, when Boomer was in the States, Ess had come to stay with her, feeling lonesome and depressed. But *still* that stare, that smile. Becoming clumsy, I asked whether Ess had revealed anything of herself, and she replied that, yes, she had several times seen Ess with nothing on, and that she was lovely. For more specific information about a rift with Boomer, she referred me to Boomer himself, implying as she did so that I thought Boomer too insensitive in personal matters to know whether there had been a rift or not. Impelled to defend him, I mentioned the dislocation Boomer had sensed, but stressed that the incompatibility was not sexual. Indeed, that Boomer seemed to perceive in Ess a quality of erotic translucency.

'I can quite imagine,' was all she would say, but the smile became a beam. Somehow, somewhere, she'd heard what she had come to hear. Inadvertently, I'd fed her the morsels she could now carry back with her to her cave.

Could Ess have been throwing herself from a high place? And to avoid capture by whom? A disquieting thought, but still I don't see how it fits.

Under that cleverness, Lois Bamford has a nasty mind. A cheap one, too. I hate the way she uses words like 'lonesome', cloyingly. Like those economists who're for ever gloating about the gravy and the jam. Anyway, from one bizarre meal to another. Boomer asked himself round to supper. I'd expected him gaunt, but he took me by surprise : dilapidated, but in good cheer. The snag is that he needs to take someone into his confidence about his love life ; and for reasons that explain themselves, has picked on me. It's all so soon ; and he's embarrassed, but not sufficiently embarrassed to engender tact. As sop to his misgivings, he moves in obliquely : talking about Ess, using her — I suppose — as a bridge from the seemly to the inevitable.

Unwisely, I told him that I'd had lunch with the Dangerous Lesbian, and that was all the excuse he needed. Although wrapping it in a good deal of circumspection, his claim is that Ess was really a homosexual too. Unlike Lois in temperament, of course. She did not want to make demands or annex. But lesbian in her special fashion, even so.

Ess, he wants me to know, was a woman who could not come to terms with the physical presence of her own body. She found it exciting to be looked at, but for a special reason. It was only then that she could conceive of her body as something impersonal. In his mind, it's all a matter of mirrors. It was through mirrors that Ess could step in amongst her own imaginings.

Such invaluable insights can only have reached Boomer through the good offices of Sister Penny. To prevent any explicit comparison of her virtues with Ess's, I tried to interest Boomer in the dealings I've been having with the Arts Council, and in the charming but totally irresponsible young lady there dispensing funds on the nation's behalf. But not a flicker. So instead, I questioned him about Ess's stay with Lois, years ago.

Evidently, it had been a bad time for them both. He'd been invited to do some work in Montreal, and without ever quite saying so they'd agreed to treat it as a trial separation. He was away six weeks. When he got back, they were quite glad to see each other, and a rift was averted.

Over there, he'd reached a temporary understanding with a conference secretary, and had lied to Ess about her, feeling justified, he said, because it had meant so little. All he can remember is the quality of her skin — sullen, he called it — and the timbre of her voice. For the life of him, he can't remember her name.

Had anything happened between Ess and Lois? He thought not. If it had, Ess would have told him, he was almost sure. It strikes me as a curious territory in which to be almost sure of anything; but Boomer's convinced. In his recollection, she was unembarrassed by her own sexual experience once it was over, and would detail it for him to any extent he seemed to need. The shame she felt was concentrated before the event, hesitating on the threshold. Unlike most of us, she had no difficulty in recovering a coherent sense of herself once it was over.

This falls short of positive proof; he admits that. But his mind's made up. And it is so because he's already committed to playing the merits of his marriage down, portraying it as greyer than it really was. The greyness could have been there all along; a dull marriage we all conspired to give a public sheen. But I doubt it. Boomer's already begun to re-write his own biography. Despite the air of buoyancy, he's begun to sound like a man denigrating the old and decent in order to legitimate the new and not so decent — a meeting of the imaginations that will be less than seemly, and could prove a cheapening tumble.

It's high time I got hold of my sister.

June 11th

I invited myself down to lunch yesterday and was snubbed. Lunch was impossible, but on second thoughts supper might be OK if I brought the wine.

I'd rather assumed that when I got down there, I'd find Boomer installed, but not so. He didn't turn up until half-past seven. Having kissed Penny decorously and waved to Sue, he enthused to me about the weather. For supper, he was ushered to his place as guest rather than as inmate. Whatever her motive, Penny's keeping him close to the path of righteousness; wisely, I can't help feeling. She doesn't feel like letting the relationship rip. But they've been to bed together; about that, I've not the slightest doubt.

Boomer pottered off at 10.30 and left the four of us to ruminate. My speculations about what the girls had noticed were answered over the washing up. Sue remarked, looking at right-angles to her line of fire, that Boomer had fallen for her Ma. I explained that this was more or less bound to happen, a consequence of his bereavement — if not strictly inevitable, at least heavily

71

determined. I also put it to her that no one was in a position to judge. We all know what we think we'll do on such occasions, but what we'll actually do is another matter. Charity is the only tenable policy.

A poor speech. Sue's glance played across me as she switched from one 90° tangent to the other. She didn't believe it, and neither did I. There's a special unpleasantness that lies in wait for uncles when they deal their nieces short. I wanted to say that I liked what was happening no better than she did, but that — charity, be buggered — I was powerless to intervene.

June 15th

Lonely when I woke up, I went for a walk on my own across the Common. Lowering myself afterwards into a chair I was seized by the muscles in the small of my back : my slipped disc providing its own punctuation.

It's a facet of Penny's conservatism that she should construe all illness as a lapse of will. Whatever his faults, Perce was never ill, and loathed being pampered. Her nurturativeness over food is quite misleading. She enjoys feeding others, but it's as an affirmation of her sense of style. It's got nothing to do with broths or poultices. Quite the reverse : 'invalid food' is one of her terms of abuse. Wincing in her armchair, I knew she'd eye me dismissively. What she'd do with me would depend on the exigencies of the moment.

A slipped disc of one's own is not amusing. And medical knowledge makes it harder to bear, not easier. It's disquieting to know that one's spinal column has ruptured, and tortured lumps of cushioning tissue are bearing on bundles of nerve fibres. Also that an operation amounts to licensing a surgeon of unspecified competence to brandish a scalpel within minute distances of your spinal cord. The collapse of so integral a part of one's skeleton is a shock of a special kind. The whole of life is predicated on the assumption that the skeleton is there to serve. That it should become a source of frailty — and of intense pain — is something new and debilitating. Ever after, the exercise of will is no longer a matter of effort, but of calculation. Of continual anxiety that the fabric will collapse under whatever strain you exert on it.

In my case, when disaster strikes, it strikes definitively. I am transfixed. Seventy-two hours in bed, flat on my back, is the only sure solution. Seventy-two hours during which I need help in standing up and sitting down; help, initially, in turning from my back on to my left or right side. And during which agency is eroded, and I become a pulp of hypochondriacal misery.

To my relief, Penny's initial distaste softened; and if not exactly solicitous, she displayed something approaching patience in getting me up the stairs and into the spare bedroom. In taking my outdoor clothes off, she even gave me a businesslike pat, as if to say that I needn't feel a fool.

Sue brought me my lunch on a tray, but I could only manage those items that could be dropped more or less vertically into my mouth. She nevertheless infused a hint of festivity into the occasion, finding my predicament a welcome diversion from Boomer and her Ma. As a more than usually generous offering of herself, she displayed the clothes she'd bought that week and was planning to take back with her to school. Taller than either of her parents, thin rather than plump, blonder than any daughter of Penny's has a right to expect, she's the personification of fetching bisexuality. The girl to make the most dedicated flit think again.

As a concession, Penny, no respecter of the GP's Sunday, summoned her long-suffering, and perhaps hopeful, Dr Glendenning. He gave me a pain-killing injection and a prescription for muscle-relaxing pills. The injection enabled me to take supper in a semi-recumbent position, and to kiss both girls goodbye before they were whisked off back to their dorms. Thereafter I fell into a troubled sleep, gin and injection working on each other unpredictably. My night was hectic. I dreamt — or did I dream? — that Boomer came in as the girls went out, and that he and Penny spent the rest of the evening carousing downstairs. Later, the whole house seemed to shake with their coitus in the double bed that Penny and Perce had once shared.

The next morning I woke late ; and there being nothing for it, got myself out of bed and along to the lavatory. En route, I heard voices downstairs. Unmistakably, one was Boomer's. I made it back to my bedroom and regained the horizontal. Penny had heard the lavatory flush, and came up to inspect. I asked what Boomer had to say for himself, but was told that he'd just 'popped in'. An unpleasant schoolboy's *double entendre* found its way into my mind, but Penny was in no mood to receive such a sally, nor I to attempt it. I told her that I had had a night of bizarre dreams in which the framework of the house had rocked to an awesome rhythm. 'The injection, John, my sweet,' she said. And added, in stage Irish, 'What a bachelor's dream, to be sure.'

Her stare, like Lois Bamford's, was friendly ; but it told me that, like Lois, she wasn't going to tell.

As I lay trying to sip coffee sideways out of a cup

74

without scalding my nose or spilling mouthfuls down my chest, other details of the night percolated back into consciousness : lavatories flushing in the small hours, the sound of laughter on the landing. The longer I lay there, the more sure I became that my dreams had been invaded by a carnal rout in the bedroom next to my own. But then I dozed ; and when I woke the sense of certainty had left me, and I was merely fuddled.

Later Penny came up to say that she had to go out, but would be back before lunch with my pills. Her mood was businesslike, and doubts were not to be entertained. For a while, I lay longing for a good cricket commentary, and then skimmed the *Financial Times*, Perce's copy that she'd not yet cancelled. The rude noises of the night's couplings filtered back again, and I felt a pang of commiseration for Perce : the attempts he had made to stake out a space for himself in this household. His *Financial Times* and squash kit. He'd avoided annihilation, but only because he was never an invalid. He must have needed Penny in all sorts of ways, but never as a child needs his parents.

The pills helped. The sun poured in through the window, and the night's animalities receded. Penny went out again, came back, brought me up a cup of tea, helped me out of bed and back again, and left me to read. At six, she appeared with a stiff gin and tonic, and at half-past with another, but didn't stay to chat ; whether because she wanted to keep me off the topic of Boomer or to prevent me relapsing into invalidhood, I couldn't make out.

Again, as soon as I'd had a bite of supper, I felt uncontrolledly drowsy ; and the dreams of the night before returned — repeating themselves with the additional confusion that I knew, as I dreamt, that I'd had the same dream the night before, and I tried to put two and two

75

together, looking for clues that would demonstrate un-
equivocally that what I was dreaming was true.

In fact, I went through the cycle twice, the first time
with two dreams to co-ordinate, the second time with
three. And the last of these became a gargantuan Holly-
wood epic: the Tower of Babel, its wall rocking and
quaking in dreadful rhythm, the landscape around it filled
with the grunts and gasps and gurgling laughter of Man
and Woman inside. Brueghel the Younger portrayed it.
Or was it Bosch? The immense Tower cracking with
the strains exerted from within, our ears deafened with the
noise. But the enterprise is inert, too. You sense the
grain of the wood of the panel on which the scene has been
painted, the cracks in the paint itself, an air of mustiness.

I lurched awake from this re-run of the Primal Scene,
lurched in fact as far as the doorway of my room — the
agonies of my back for the moment abated. My door was
ajar, and without question, the house was empty. Quite
still. There was a solitary light in the hallway downstairs.
Penny's bedroom door was open, and her bed empty.
Sweating, I made my way along the landing to the
lavatory and passed water, not because I particularly
needed to, but as my passport back to the world of the
everyday. The lavatory's flush echoed through the house,
echoing all the lavatory flushes there had ever been.

On my way back down the landing, I reflected un-
happily on the symbolism of the tower; the Tower of
Babel, *La Tour d'Ivoire*. Impurity and purity. The profane
and the sterile. However valiantly we struggle to cope
with life in its own terms, the imagination stubbornly
returns us to these two polar extremities, and the tyranny
of their metaphors. Towers that are enclosures, and enclosures that're towers. The familiar tower that contains

us, hidden, during the day ; and then the alien tower, with its scarcely concealed obscenities, that we watch from outside while we're asleep.

Comforted by these reflections, I settled back into my lair. The time, I was surprised to see, was only a quarter past midnight.

Cleansed of symbolic odds and ends, I fell deeply asleep, and then, just before waking the next morning, had the dream that had been lying in wait for me all along. My bid for liberation.

I was back in the mortuary, but the atmosphere of horror was gone. The drawer opened as before. But when the attendant pulled the shroud back from Ess's face, he pulled it from her almost completely, leaving only a corner draped over her ankles, hiding her feet.

She was still, of course, but it was Ess as I knew her, and I could take her in : free to back-track and compare in a way that you can't in the presence of someone more ordinarily sentient. She was alive in the sense that Weston's photographs of his mistresses are : Weston, whose nudes knock modern art into a bucket. Classical, but with every blemish recorded ; definitive, but also a shade perverse. For a while, she was another Weston ; a plate in a collection I hadn't yet come across. But then, herself again. Her body was more compact than I'd foreseen. Rather than two masses — rib cage and pelvis — jointed at the waist, her torso formed a coherent volume, its surface, from sternum on down, a single uninflected sweep. I could ensure that I understood the placing of her breasts in relation to her chest, and her nipples to her breasts : widely placed, and pointing somewhat outwards, not straight forward like the headlamps of a car.

My dream then transformed itself into an exercise in

77

geometry. I was able to verify that, as I hoped, her breasts and nipples, in pointing outwards, lay on lines drawn as radii from her spine; and that these radii were themselves at right-angles to one another, intersecting at her spinal cord. This principle of physiological organisation became the focus of intense personal pride. It linked the realms of nature and mathematics as poignantly as does the Golden Section. Ken Clark's *The Nude* gives instances: a tritoness of Scopas's, a girl at her ease in the lower left-hand corner of Titian's 'Bacchanal', even Goya's Maja.

Vertically down Ess's stomach lay the scar of the operation that had rendered her infertile. The body of a woman, not a girl. Her pubic hair was an echo of the hair on her head; the red a shade less chestnut, and flecked with grey, arranged not as a neat delta, but more as a crescent, running like her scar vertically to the plain of her body — an arrangement that offered her nothing by way of disguise.

I woke entirely soothed: one of those rare occasions when the elements of your interior life fall back into place, and you're left for the time being with the illusion of belonging.

At peace with the wraiths that normally haunt my awakenings, I watched the sunlight in the leaves of the rowan outside my window. After a while, there were sounds of stirring downstairs; and Penny, source of so much perplexity, brought me up my cup of tea. Noticing that I was no longer sorry for myself, she settled on the bed's edge, while I retailed to her the Tower of Babel story, though suppressing the one about Ess. I also remarked on the emptiness of the house. She restricted herself to saying that she'd been round to keep Boomer company. Her tone was businesslike: that of a nurse

78

allocated to look after a new patient, one with a paper skull. But her mood is up rather than down. The signs are that Boomer's devotion is good for her morale. 'Morale' is the word that comes to mind, though ; she's not in love, nor in the least danger of becoming so.

The time had come, I judged, to rise from my bed of pain and get back to St John's Wood and the comfort of my steel-boned corset. Penny's patience in such matters is not to be tested : as soon as you can move, you're expected to do so.

June 21st

Idyllic weather, and misgivings recede of their own accord. Echoes of Babel are fainter ; and I've accommodated myself, I find, to the idea that Penny and Boomer are carrying on. It'll probably do them both good. Boomer's inexperienced, and Penny's mood is not her own ; but there's comfort in her determination that Boomer must observe the proprieties, and relief for me in the discovery that I'm included among those for whom a front of respectability is going to be maintained.

June 23rd

Yesterday, one of my trips to Oxford. It's curious how welcoming academic institutions are to outsiders like myself. We don't disrupt the jealousies, but are close enough to offer a sympathetic ear.

My supper was partially spoilt by a female sociologist whose name I didn't quite catch : mid-forties, with a mouth like a gin-trap. She launched into a sustained attack on, of all people, Boomer. I'm astonished that their worlds should overlap; and, even if they did, that he should get so badly on her nerves. They crossed each other as experts on a Civil Service committee to do with the prefabrication of council houses. She sees Boomer as an uncouth engineer who's trespassing, and leaving muddy footprints. Looking at her tight little face, I put her down as power-hungry, doing battle for Social Science and her own immediate interest. The bursar, whom I rather like, told me afterwards that this unappealing lady had recently married and is generally thought to be charming. The rage of her ambition, however, is not in question.

I itched to tell her that Boomer Mulloy was my sister's lover; but contented myself with passing on the news, over coffee, that he was recently bereaved. For a second, the ring of creases around the gin-trap relaxed, and a slight flush found its way on to two grey cheeks. Ageing gamin, she then enunciated softly, but with meticulous care, the two phrases 'How unfortunate', and 'His poor wife', doing so in such a way as to convey her own indelible righteousness.

Marginally embarrassed, she slipped away into the chair next to the Principal's, to forward her career by more direct means. I was left to eavesdrop on a conversation as keen as it was costive, between three late-middle-aged women who would sooner have lost a limb than expose themselves to justified criticism in a matter of verbal nicety. It was about the precise meaning and derivation of the word 'coruscate'. And then its sequel: a conversation about the precise meaning and derivation of the word 'blanco' — either Low German I seem to recall, or Romance. At one point, it seemed that they might stray on to better ground, but they sheered away in time. The question arose of why 'dapper' can only be used of a man, and if of a woman implies that she is lesbian. And of why 'statuesque' can only be used of a woman. Appropriately academic innuendoes were exchanged, but nothing more. Afterwards, I asked one if she'd ever committed a verbal gaff. She thought not, at least since she was a child. She prefers to work within a vocabulary she can command totally. As if to reassure us both, she did add that, after all, the scope of that etymological tyranny of hers is not inconsiderable.

Getting back this morning, whom should I find on my doorstep but Boomer. I still find it hard to imagine him earning that sociological lady's execrations. I mentioned her to him, and cast a shadow by so doing. He looked as though he might say something impatient, but merely wrinkled up his nose and gestured vaguely, dismissively, at thin air. Instinctively, I feared more confidences, and was right.

He suggested a pub lunch out of doors, and led me down to the banks of the Thames, to a terrace teeming with just the sort of arty fraud I would have assumed he loathes. Returning with our pints, ducking as he did so around the elbow of a Red Indian sculptress, he set off for the second time along his dangerous tangent. This time, his proposition was that Ess had really been frigid. I don't like quarrelling, least of all with the bereaved, but this struck me as inconsistent and vulgar to boot. Ess's death and the discovery of Penny's body seem to have transformed him from a man of due reticence into a lobotomised boor.

But even in his present state, he had enough tact to

detect my hostility, and drew back. Just in case he felt like pressing on none the less, I told him he was bloody lucky to have had a woman he could idealise at all. That in comparison to Ess's, most women's bodies are chunks of flesh over which they exercise property rights. And that there are even some who only exercise those in the hope that they'll act as a titillation or bait.

Boomer apologised and we were friends again, surviving our trip to the water's edge without another mishap. He'd read, in Pepys' diary I think, that after twenty years of marriage, a man is lucky if he can distinguish the touch of his wife's flesh from the touch of his own. He was interested in the idea that, with time and familiarity, husbands and wives come to fuse their body images. But he was only being polite. Neither of us wanted to talk about body images. It was a route back on to safer ground ; and we made it smoothly enough, via professional users of their bodies — dancers, gymnasts — and out on to the secure pastures of sport. I avoided the depression that this scatty conversation would otherwise have caused by a stroke of luck.

I had fallen to brooding on the wretchedness of those Oxford spinsters as expressions of the Scholarly Ideal, and on whether they were more or less wretched in their own way than the art élite all around us, when, at a near-by table, I spied a distinctly foxy-looking Jimmy Quist. And with him, young Persephone. He introduced Persephone to Boomer, and reintroduced her to me. We chatted then split up, Boomer making off towards Penny, while Jimmy, Persephone and I went back towards St John's Wood with the intention of watching some cricket. But Persephone proved averse, so the three of us strolled in the Park, scuffing our feet on the parched turf, with Nash's cornices peering out at us through the trees. A Universal Pictures back lot, now littered with every sort of debris under the sun; even a broken bicycle chain, a contraceptive, and an abandoned high-heel shoe.

Persephone's on the brink of falling for Jimmy, I'd judge; but he seems to find her too young. Twenty-two or three I take her to be; an age at which young women, from the vantage point of the forties, can look dangerously like children. She walks in a curiously dishevelled way. On the other hand, she's wonderfully clean, and that's a virtue. She also reminds me strongly of Ess. It's an air of self-sufficiency they have in common, I think.

Jimmy was being affable. He showed no sign of wanting to make off with her on his own. On the contrary, every sign of a conflict of interest: wanting to deflect Persephone on to someone else, and seeing me as a candidate; but wanting, too, to keep the door ajar. Also he wanted to talk about Ess; and this in the end is what we did.

He explained that Boomer's wife had just died, conceding to me as he did so that if you didn't know, you could hardly have guessed. Ess, he said, had always struck him as someone special. We talked for a while about the affair she might or might not have been having with Perce. This struck Jimmy as quite implausible: credible only if you did not know them. It seems that some months ago, she paid Jimmy a visit, ostensibly to ask his advice about something she'd written. She was half-way through a novel I'd heard nothing about: a languorous piece about a girl's upbringing in the tropics. It reminded Jimmy of Jean Rhys; not to his taste, but publishable all the same. He distanced himself, spoofing Ess's offering as 'Oh, you know, pubescent-girl-in-eroticised-landscape', but admitted that he found touching the thought of all this bubbling away inside Ess's head.

I provided something facile about how very sly of her it was to be writing away in secret like that; and remembered as I did so that 'sly' was the word Penny had used. 'Austere'? 'Sly'? Probably she was neither. Rather, we misread her, and now are perplexed because she followed her own course.

Hurt that she had shown her manuscript to him rather than to me, I asked whether he'd kept it. It seems not. He sent it back more or less immediately, and assumes that it's sitting there somewhere on Ess's desk, Boomer still being too taken up with the rediscovery of life's meaning to come across it.

Although he expresses himself obliquely, Jimmy seems as upset by Boomer's present state of mind as I am. Looking at Boomer, you've the impression that the components of an amiable personality have dropped apart, and that for the time being he's an assortment of unruly odds and ends. Bereavement's probably like this more often than I realise; but in Jimmy and myself he's certainly alienating two potentially sympathetic friends.

It wasn't Ess as an authoress that Jimmy wanted to talk about, in any case. He'd something else to get off his chest.

Apparently, while Jimmy and Ess were locked in literary discussion, Beeb had wandered into the room in her dressing gown. She'd got out of a bath, and had come down partly to say hello to Ess, and partly to ask Jimmy what she should wear. For all practical purposes, she had nothing on. Later, when she'd got dressed, they fell to chatting in an animated way about the function of clothes — not as a protection, a barrier against the outside world, but as a barrier between our compromised, anxious every-day selves and the sunlit selves we long to become. Beeb had been reading *Love's Body*, or so Jimmy claimed, and was holding forth on the tyranny of commonsense as it expresses itself in clothes.

Beeb's blessed with the kind of body that finds its way into the Pirelli Calendar. Blithely Californian. Ess had said it was fine for Beeb, but if you look embarrassed without your clothes, it wouldn't do at all. They then waxed philosophical, puzzling over how something public, like showing your body to other people, can be so bound up with something private: the individual's discovery of herself, and where, for her, the boundary between the safe and the orgiastic finally seems to lie.

Jimmy's sure that, as they chatted, Ess was experiencing an impulse to take off her clothes, then and there. They'd all been drinking, and he's convinced that, if he hadn't been there, she would have done just that. She kept fingering the buttons of her blouse, as if one part of her were subverting the other half's better judgment.

They also talked about see-throughs. Beeb thought they were lovely, more or less whoever wore them. Ess would have loved to wear them too, but thought of all those males eyes and was daunted. If she were still twenty, yes; but at forty, she'd missed the boat.

I was about to mention my Ess dream when, as a matter of courtesy, Jimmy turned to Persephone and asked what she thought. He'd meant 'Would you, Persephone, wear a see-through?' But she replied, as I suspect Ess would have replied, on behalf of someone else:

'She wouldn't have worn one, even if she were twenty.'

The obliqueness intrigues me. I don't think I've met

anyone of less than twenty-five who would put themselves automatically in someone else's place in quite that way.

And, as it happens, I think she's right. Looking back from forty to twenty, Ess would have imagined herself a pace-setter. But she was forgetting her perennial caution. Reconstructing Ess's reconstruction of herself as a forward-looking twenty-year-old seemed a surprisingly natural thing to do. Caught up in this curious resurrection, I discovered that I had been staring more fixedly than was proper at Persephone's breasts; not firmly encased, as Ess's would have been, but soft and slightly jumbled, like the rest of her.

But young Persephone's physique isn't my immediate concern. I must get hold of Boomer and rattle him into searching for Ess's manuscript. At the very least, it'll make a seemlier topic of conversation between us than comparisons of his deceased wife's charms with my sister's.

June 24th

Written down, Jimmy's account of his visit from Ess looks far-fetched; make-believe, even. Why do I accept it? Because I trust his manner, I suppose: normally so reticent, his occasional confidences create an air of authenticity. It could be that his make-believings about Ess and mine have fallen into the same archetypal groove. The fantasies of men about women. But even if that's so, actuality and archetypical fantasy do seem to be parallelling each other rather closely for the time being.

And I do rather miss that hour or two watching cricket with him. Spectating at a cricket match is like worrying at a hole in a tooth with your tongue: inherently unrewarding but hard to stop. But if you spectate with Jimmy, hidden meanings sometimes surface. We once met by accident in the Members' Stand, by no means the priapic spot its name suggests, and without realising who he was, watched the best batsman in the world put the local bowlers to the sword. This bronze barbarian took all the risks that the shrewd and mortal learn not to take, and as he did so brought back to life the fantasy systems of *Rover* and *Hotspur*, whole and unharmed. Once, with a wrist flick, he lifted the ball to land with sickening force beside a Member so senile that he'd slept through the performance from the beginning. To have waited seventy years, dreaming about the hitters of yesteryear, Jessop and Percy Fender; to have the dream become solid flesh and bone before your eyes. And to be asleep! A sad and almost lethal irony. We spent some time huddled in a Wimpy Bar, devising a set of rules that would make routine cricket better to watch. A doomed venture, I suppose, because the redeeming beauties of any sport evolve unforeseeably — like the quarterback's pass in American football, biologically impossible unless you've seen it occur.

After a while, we found we'd reinvented baseball, a game neither of us enjoys. All the same, it's typical of Jimmy that he should spend so long trying to redesign a set of rules in order to achieve a better fit between convention and our need for moments of surprise.

June 29th

Penny invited us all down to supper: Jimmy and Beeb, myself, Boomer of course, and Persephone too — whether at Beeb's instigation or Jimmy's, I'm still not sure. Granted the realities, Boomer ought to have been host, but Penny insisted on treating him as a guest, on a footing with the rest of us ; although a guest whom she felt free every now and again to scold. Persephone had been placed next to me, so that we might strike up an understanding, and was separated from Jimmy by the length of the table. Again I was struck by the echo of Ess : it was momentarily like having her there again at my elbow.

Boomer looked strained. The buoyancy's still there, but it's complicated now by some pain as yet to be specified. Penny's recovered, on the other hand. She's not gay, but the rudiments of gaiety are there, waiting to assemble themselves into a living performance.

Beeb filled in the cracks with a round of chatter about the new Sainsbury's. And with her physical presence. As if recapturing the theme of an earlier conversation, she'd come to do Ess's memory proud in a white cotton shirt. Designed to reach down almost to her ankles, it revealed her — a massive gold toque apart — as comfortably naked. The competition for Jimmy's rheumy gaze, Persephone was being reminded, was going to be formidable.

As our consommé reached the table, reeking of madeira, it occurred to me that I've not yet spoken to Penny about cash. About how that consommé is going to be paid for, and a good deal else besides. An extraordinary omission. Her outgoings are heavy, and she's not the best-equipped woman in the world to effect economies. Pa has probably said something, but I doubt whether effective communication has taken place.

Consommé was followed by a vulgar-looking concoction of artichokes, and Beeb held forth about her nephews' ailments, which she attributes to the evil vibrations of the military-industrial complex. She seemed happy to fill in for Penny, supplying ebullience where she would normally stay quiet.

But we were a roomful waiting for someone else to raise the forbidden topic of Ess and Perce. We reached it sooner than I would have thought possible, via the innocuous question of men coping for themselves. Beeb went out into the kitchen to help Penny with the steak, and on their return they began to interrogate the three of us about how we managed. My status as a bachelor was high. In my own way, I obviously cope; though Boomer cited my taste for rum fudge and bitter as evidence that bachelordom leads to eccentricity. It was revealed that Jimmy could not cope at all. His virtuosity in keeping unlikely ménages alive was a skill conceived from a desperate desire to avoid having to cook. As a young man with elder sisters, he had never had to learn. Neither as a student, nor ever after. Boomer's position, it seemed was marginal: he tries, but lacks skill; the kind of housekeeper who's accident-prone, cracking every egg he boils.

Penny said this peevishly, as if it were Boomer's fault that more than eggs had recently been broken. The air prickled. Dangerous questions were to be embarked on. Only Penny or Boomer could license us in talking about Ess and Perce, and Boomer was already looking ruffled, as if he'd been knocked around a bit. My sister is not in the least a bitch, still less an assassin. But I've noticed that as she becomes engaged in a relation with a man, she is liable to lay about herself without regard.

'Perce,' she announced, 'was hopeless too.' But this verdict she expressed without a trace of the dismissiveness with which, all these years, she has characterised Perce, to his face and behind his back. The blame once focused on

89

him is now to be historically diffused. Henceforth, it's to rest not on Perce, but on the women who brought him up. And only on them as the pawns of those ranting preachers who have convinced Scots down the years of the virtues of cleanliness and the servile status of women.

But where was the step that would lead us to Perce and Ess together? We didn't have long to wait or wonder. Penny's next move carried us the whole way home. Janey had flu last term, and Penny had to go down to the school to see her. She'd been on the point of leaving Perce to fend for himself, something she did rarely, when Ess stepped into the breach. Ess insisted that they say nothing to Perce, and that it should all come as a surprise. When he got back that evening, it was Ess who was waiting for him with his meal, not Penny. Perce was tickled pink.

Watching Boomer, it was clear that it was as much news to him as it was to me. It must have been a night when he was on one of his trips, and Ess was alone. I could picture the mood Ess would have created, stage-managing the occasion so that Perce had to accept it as a piece of theatre he couldn't question. Changing places in that way would have suited perfectly Ess's taste for the theatrical. She would have carried it off as a friendly but slightly disconcerting tease.

Deceived in thought if not in deed, Boomer sat piecing together the implications. How far had Ess carried her impersonation — how thorough-going was the swap? And how late had she stayed? Was it conceivable that her portrayal of the good wife had extended to sharing Perce's bed? If she hadn't mentioned it to him, it must have been too trivial to be worth remembering, or too fraught to be brought to light.

Boomer took the full force of the blow, but I felt its weight, and so did Jimmy. Only Beeb hadn't seen it struck; Beeb, and perhaps Persephone. But all of us were cast for a few moments into the silence that Penny's cleaver left behind it. Once again it was Beeb who did her best to darn up the fabric of amity. But unfortunately, her efforts led straight from one zone of delicacy to another:

'Ess poor darling. You know, she was writing a book...'

The transition was cushioned by the Caribbean comfort of her body; and also, more obliquely, by her intonation, wholly unmodified since those afternoons she and Evie had spent together as girls at the point-to-point. It was a sensitive area, none the less; and Boomer was obliged to to commit himself.

He mumbled something about how it had all come in a rush, and how vivid it was. Jimmy supported him, and the adjective 'austere' crept in again: the label we hang round her memory like a dog's name-tag. But wasn't she austere only in the sense that a pane of glass is? What you saw through that pane wasn't austere. Her father had spoken of a passionate nature; and on reflection, that seemed nearer the mark than either Jimmy's efforts, or Penny's cynicism. Perhaps, in the fastnesses of her imagination, Ess had 'wanted a screw', as my sister so daintily put it. Even, for some inexplicable reason, with Perce. Or with just anyone. But her sense of style would have required her to tidy that impulse up a good deal before she came to act on it.

Beeb's mind seemed to have been working along an analogous path, but all she said was: 'Not really austere, was she? I'd always thought she must be rather gorgeous.' She's no voyeur. She just thinks Ess was lovely, and that's the end of it.

Meanwhile, Boomer's position was horrible. Penny was knocking him about, semi-publicly, and with enough sharpness of intent to warn him of worse to follow. The longer he leaves it, trying to conciliate Penny, the weaker his position's going to become. On the other hand, he's in love, and in no mood to do battle, with Penny least of all. Outsiders like Jimmy, Beeb and myself could offer him anchorage during the dark nights ahead, but he's cut off from us more or less completely by his fervour.

And Sister Penny's in no mood to relent. If she had the elbowroom, she wouldn't use it. When she struck her next stake into the ground, it was with a good trouper's brave gaiety:

'Well, she bowled poor Perce over. They were off to make a night of it.'

If you didn't know her well, Penny might have seemed like someone doing her damnedest to make the grim seem tolerable: buckling herself to the discipline of the show going on. But there was an edge to her voice. She'd pushed her luck with Boomer too far, too soon; and knew it. She's probably more rattled than she's realised; and although he's an innocent in the arts of sexual infighting, he's a survivor even so. Perceiving that she'd played an old game in a new and inappropriate context, she made an affectionate gesture towards him, reaching across to touch his hand. But too late. His cheeks were bright red, and his voice crackled as though it might do one of its squeaks:

'That's crap, as you perfectly well know.'

Penny was immediately conciliatory. What she was offering, for the first time, was evidence that they were having an affair, and that he was someone special to her. Boomer levelled out. They weren't going to have a public row, but he'd more to say before he stopped. Penny is not going to reduce him to rubble, using Ess as a weapon ; and she was wise to give ground. He wanted to know whether she had evidence for her claim ; whether by any chance she had another well-placed surprise in store.

I could scarcely believe it : Penny looked as though she might cry. According to the old, old rules, her next move was to tell Boomer not to get wrought up ; she was only joking. But the water was deep, and her face had on it an expression almost of pleading ; one that, to the best of my knowledge, it never in the whole of her life bore before.

Beeb then took a hand. She said again what a lovely person Ess had been, and that it was a crime to disagree over her. And Jimmy weighed in, demonstrating for Persephone's benefit that he and Beeb operated as a unit in times of stress, asking Boomer about Ess's manuscript, where it was. Boomer rubbed his hands over his face as though he were suddenly very tired, apologised for sounding off, and said that he didn't know. He expected it was in Ess's study at home, but it wasn't anywhere obvious or he would have seen it. The while, Penny sat red-eyed and shaken. And then, bending over to kiss Boomer as she did so, she made her way out to the kitchen, in search of second helpings.

Jimmy and I wittered for a minute or two about books, eventually coming to roost on Irene Handl's *The Sioux*, which I like and he doesn't. Persephone joined it ; she's read it too. And I was then free to catch Boomer's eye, and to brood on what he'd meant by a 'well-placed surprise'. He could well have had in mind Penny's revelation about Ess changing places. But I thought not ; something about his phrasing suggested a surprise that was more concrete — that could be well-placed in the literal sense. It was a second before two and two slipped together. Penny had urged me to leave Ess's holdall and its ambiguous contents with her. My guess was that she'd shown it to Boomer at a judicious moment. Or, more likely, that she'd allowed him to stumble across it, parked somewhere around the house.

He'd have been deeply injured. I'm sure he's talked to no one except Penny about Ess and Perce. He'll have fallen in love with her because he needed a listener he he could trust. If only he'd had the wit to pick on me! And he could well have talked about Ess incessantly to Penny: on and on into the night, in that tone of his that almost amounted to eulogy. That first night, when they had gone to bed together, trying to find some comfort, Boomer would have talked about Ess as they got undressed, and talked about Ess as he lay back after it was over. Ess, Ess: it would have lacerated Penny's pride. She'd loathe being a substitute for anyone in bed, even someone just dead. In all probability, that first night, Boomer scarcely noticed who Penny was. At the time, she'd have been compassionate; but it will all have been credit that sooner or later he'll have to repay.

After the initial shock, Boomer had probably worked his way through to the same balance of doubts about Ess's holdall as I had. He would have recognised the white cotton nightie. And would no doubt have been introduced by Penny to Perce's miserable packet of condoms. I can catch just the note of hilarity she would have struck in doing it. But he would also have seen the books they'd packed, and been marginally reassured by them. *If*, that is, Penny had seen fit to leave those books in place. The thought crossed my mind — leaving a trail of slime as it did so — that she might just have put them on a shelf, and said nothing. Boomer could well have spouted forth his praises of Ess at moments that were *disastrously* ill-chosen. And Penny exacts her revenge; you're not someone's twin for forty years without knowing that about them. The absent-minded removal of those two books would have been her style to a tee.

Discovering that I was stalled, I drifted back, I remember, into the conversation about books. Persephone's innocence about the written word was an anodyne I felt urgent need of. She's young enough to believe that books are important for what's written inside them. They're objects on which you allow your critical faculties to play. It matters to her, in detail, what the characters in a book like *The Sioux* say. But to those of us already too old for them, all conversations about what one person in a book says to another person in a book are quite unmemorable. When she's forty, perhaps she'll surprise herself with an effusion every bit as unexpected as Ess's. Listening to her talk, I turned over in my mind the question of what she'd find she'd written about. And who she then would be.

In Jimmy's comments there was the same nostalgia. His first thoughts on scanning Ess's manuscript at full professional speed would have been those of someone who found her appealing; and it will have been the dissonance between the inner and outer Ess that caught his attention, alerting him to that hand of hers, fumbling abstractedly with the buttons of her blouse.

Penny's system of hospitality is unremitting, and by the time we'd tottered off into the sitting room for our coffee, she and Boomer had papered over the cracks. He was allowed to dispense the Cointreau. But watching him do it, I was sure he'd been an idiot. Through a series of accidents and flukes, he's committed to a relationship within which he's now doomed to fight for his life. Wholly unproductively. He's tough — that I don't doubt; but it's the toughness of desperation. On the way through to the last ditch, he's going to take a mauling. Penny'll sustain injuries, too; ones that'll transform her, irreversibly, from feeling young to feeling old.

For the moment, though, all was well. She dumped herself down on the sofa and pulled him down next to her, pressing herself against him. The immediate outlook was good. She'd realised that she needed him, and was no longer pretending to the rest of us that she didn't. In the short run, she'd be generous, abundantly. But sooner or later, the cracks would reopen. For each of them it is their last chance; the last serious attempt that either will make to establish something based on love. And they'll botch it.

Feeling melancholic, I left early, hugging them both. I'd made my adieux to the others when I remembered my undertaking to drop Persephone off at Swiss Cottage on my way home. She didn't seem taken aback by my neglect, and we drove back into Town chatting about this and that; a soothing coda to a disquieting evening.

Soothing, and also fitting. Her arrival on the scene seems to have signalled a shift in the momentum of events. Not just their tempo, but their underlying tone. She's provided conceptual punctuation, rather in the way that my slipped disc provided punctuation of a physical sort. And it's apt enough that the conceptual and physical should be slightly out of registration; a typewritten semicolon that leaves a double impression on the page.

It's as if we've moved back from the regime of disaster, where events and moods hit you out of the blue, to approximate normality, where there's a sense of predictability and steady incremental flow. From tsunami to the ordinary swell and break of rollers. Since her arrival, emotions have seemed more content to unfold themselves at an intelligible rate.

July 3rd

More idyllic weather. Reassured once more that my misgivings are pointless. Penny and Boomer are made for each other. They ought to marry soon, and be each other's consolation. If there are interventions to be made, they're matters of looping up a thread here, disentangling a knot there. All could be as well as marriages ever are.

July 4th

Penny rang. All does seem well ; she sounds as though she's glowing. I tried talking about Boomer, but she cut me off at once : 'Don't *speak* about it. Just cross your fingers ... ' It'd take a thick-thumbed mechanic to interfere in the face of that.

I have pressed Boomer about Ess's manuscript, though. Spurred by my nagging, he's looked but found nothing. She might have thrown it away. Or sent it off to another friend for advice. But whom ?

The third time I rang him, Boomer was fishing around at the other end of the line, trying to ask me a favour but not knowing how to frame it. It turns out, two favours. And in his best style, he got to the major via the minor ; the worry at the centre of his mind via one at its periphery :

'It's a lovely girl, that Persephone.' While my mind was elsewhere at Penny's supper table, she'd engaged Boomer in a high-flown conversation, asking him a lot of questions none of which he could answer. Someone had told her that Nietzsche had once earned a living as a professor of philology. Was that true? All Boomer could remember about Nietzsche was that he'd once seen a photograph of him with his mistress: he was pulling a hand-cart and she was brandishing a whip. Was it true that Nietzsche stood the hermeneutic enterprise on its head? — the Sign now construed not as Performatory Utterance, but as the Dead Residue of Struggle. And was it true that British philosophers have thought of the Sign as opaque, whereas Nietzsche conceived of it as translucent — a glass through which we peer darkly, trying to descry the lineaments of its own palaeontology? (Or something equally startling, to the same general effect!)

Had I played a practical joke? Had I perhaps told Persephone that Boomer was a philosopher rather than a humble engineer? Obviously something had gone wrong, but I reassured him that it was none of my doing. And my grasp of modern semiotics being roughly co-extensive with Boomer's, we relapsed into a conversation more suited to our age and station: the likelihood that Persephone was drawn to Jimmy.

Normally, Boomer would not have noticed any such vibration. Love must have altered the range of his perceptual field. We were agreed, too, that Beeb had been looking magnificent. Ready to repel boarders. We then embarked on the sort of conversation I occasionally have with Jimmy, but which, for Boomer, was totally out of character: about how men dress up in the face of a threat while women undress. We put on armour while they take it off. And how different it must feel if your body itself is your security: as it is, but artfully adorned.

However, Boomer was filling in time, trying to build a

bridge to what he really needed to say. A gulp at the other
end of the line, and he made it at last. He wants to know
whether I'll go round and help him sort out Ess's papers.
Naturally, I'll be happy to. Had Penny helped with Ess's
clothes? It seems not; when the moment came, she felt
like a grave-robber, and couldn't. There are thousands of
blouses and scarves, and I agreed with Boomer that it
would be a crime to pack them off to Oxfam. Attempting
an uneasy jocularity, I suggested that it might be a task
for the Dangerous Lesbian; but to my dismay, he took
the idea seriously, and wanted me to ring her then and
there. Recalling her filleting of me, a re-match with Lois
in the context of Ess's underwear was a prospect I shied
away from. I put it to him, somewhat hastily, that we
give her a miss.

The pun, unintentional though it was, struck me as
funny: but try as I might, I couldn't get him to see the
point of it.

July 7th

Anyway, give her a miss we did. Last night, I bustled
round to Boomer's, dispatched him for fish and chips, and
settled myself to reconnoitre.

Ess had had a small study to herself, and was tidy, to
the extent of having a filing system. The tidiness was
deceptive however. She was the kind of person who sets
up a system of classification with some care, but can bring
herself to use it only sporadically. Meanwhile letters,
papers from the Bureau, bills, memos were stacked in
trays as they came to hand. It was Ess who dealt with all
the household bills. Even Boomer's tax returns. But it's

going to be quite a labour to disentangle the detritus of these activities one from the other.

My instinct was to flip through in search of literary clues, and then throw the rest out unexamined. Propriety forbade this. In any case, evidence of literary effort was harder to find than I'd foreseen. A letter from Jimmy was all I came across. It picked up what was presumably a thread of argument from earlier letters about how her novel might be recast to make it more commercially acceptable. I scanned the letter for evidence of Jimmy's special interest in her, but found only his usual felicitous economy of phrase. Friendly, encouraging; but nothing more. He hid his lack of interest in what Ess had written with a skill I can only admire.

But of the manuscript itself, not a sign. Nor were there even rough notes or typed out quotations. Nothing. The three natty filing cases revealed nothing beyond wadges of insurance policies and household receipts.

When Boomer got back, I cross-questioned him. Ess hadn't shown him the story at all, wanting to hold it back until finished, and then to try it out on him complete. He knew she was typing it, but pretended not to take too much interest, lest he disrupt her flow.

Some months ago, she'd told him she was stuck. It was then she'd shown it to Jimmy. But slowly she'd seemed to regain a certain momentum. Could it be upstairs somewhere? Possibly but he doubted it. We could look. She could have tried it out on someone else, but who? Boomer could think of no one but the omnipresent Lois. She *was* a possibility. But if she had the manuscript, why hadn't she mentioned it to me when we'd last spoken? Could Ess have torn the lot up and thrown it away, rough workings and all? Anything's possible, Boomer thought.

She might have despaired of it suddenly while he was away this last time, and chucked it into the boiler, but it seemed unlikely.

That left us with the search upstairs. Boomer walked round the house, pointing out to me the likely places, while I did the investigating, delving in a cupboard here, a chest of drawers there. Boomer, I noticed, had moved out of the room he had shared with Ess, and was camping in their spare room. But his bed didn't look as though it had been slept in for some time. The last site for investigation was the chest of drawers beside what used to be their double bed. Boomer hovered around while I went through the drawers, starting at the top and working down. There was a heartbreaking array of pants and bras, mostly ecru or brown, and almost all with lace frills. At the back of a drawer filled with silk scarves, some of which I recognised, and nestling against a cache of tampons, I came across what I'd been looking for. A brown manilla envelope. But before I'd opened it, I knew it wasn't the right shape. Inside were photos. Not glossily professional ; just the usual family snaps. Boomer taken by Ess. Ess taken by Boomer. Occasionally Ess and Boomer together, taken by someone else. A sad commentary on the childless state that they so often appeared on their own.

Not a damned thing ! We sat on the bed and waited for inspiration. Obviously, the next step was to phone Lois ; but if she has it, she may well intend to hang on to it, and faced with a straight question, might deny all knowledge. In a way that's alien to me, I fell to the calculation of ways and means, rehearsing a trade-off that I could offer Lois : Ess's manuscript in exchange for Ess's clothes. It couldn't be put that bluntly ; but if it wasn't presented with a fair degree of resolution, there was nothing to prevent her carrying off the clothes and hanging on to the manuscript.

My nerve steeled to this absurdity, I proposed to Boomer that we ring her and that I should act on his behalf. The exchange proved delicate. I asked whether she'd be willing to help Boomer sort out poor Ess's effects: her papers, her clothes, all the loose ends. Reminding her of Ess's exquisite taste in such matters, I told her of wardrobes full of skirts and suits, dozens of pairs of shoes, and drawers resplendent with underwear.

We agreed that it would be unthinkable to make an Oxfam bundle of the whole array. Lois offered to come over and cope — 'just say the word'. I then went on to the question of the papers. I'd had a look: some were Bureau papers that I'd be happy to sort out and bundle for her. In return, could she quiet Boomer's worries on a particular point. Did she know that Ess had been writing a novel; and could she help us find it? She admitted hearing about it from Ess, but had never seen it. Ess had offered to show it to her and she had expressed eagerness; but assumes that in the end Ess got cold feet.

Lois did suggest that Ess might have left her manuscript somewhere in the Bureau, and that she'd happily have a look for me on Monday. And meanwhile, wouldn't I like some help with all those clothes: it hardly sounded a job for two men.

I told her that I'd prefer to get things settled one at a time. First the manuscript, then the clothes. I came off the telephone sweating with the strain; Lois Bamford would have made a small fortune for herself negotiating commercial contracts. She hasn't committed herself; and in all probability that manuscript is sitting on her desk at this very moment, within arm's reach.

July 8th

Padding round that empty house with Boomer, sitting at the desk Ess had sat at, shuffling through the bills and letters she'd shuffled through, I'd no sense of Ess herself. From now on, she'll exist in the imagination or not at all. I've never had so clear and definitive a sense of her deadness. More so by far than seeing her dead in the flesh. Her routine is devoid of meaning without the person herself there to inform it. She's more nearly alive reflected in the unsuspecting Persephone than she is now in her own study or bedroom. Dead as the lies that Lois and I have been telling each other over a memento of Ess that neither of us, any longer, has an adequate reason for wanting. Boomer is in the same boat. It is not the eloquence of Ess's objects that's upsetting him, but precisely their lack of eloquence.

July 9th

It was a relief when a call came through from Lois, just before lunch, to say that she'd looked round the Bureau and found nothing. Could I suggest anywhere else? I couldn't, so we left it at that. To this minute, I don't know whether she has that manuscript by her or not. And to my surprise, she made no mention of Ess's garments. Perhaps for her, too, unseemly excitement has died away, leaving queasiness in its wake.

Staring at my blotter over a melancholy mid-afternoon cup of tea, my negotiation with Lois began to seem positively sordid. What had we been haggling over? Ess's manuscript, and Ess's clothes. Inner and outer surface: the two efforts Ess had made to be seen.

No wonder our negotiations have gone sour. What's worse, Boomer and I still have her possessions on our hands, and philosophising about love's magic body won't help disperse them. Yet just before five, I had an inspiration : Beeb and Evie. Class would tell. Whilst sorrowing over Ess, they'd subsume the whole business of dispersal to the terms of reference of the country house sale. They would not just cope ; they would do so in good style.

July 15th

This morning, Beeb, Evie and I packed Boomer off round the corner to see Penny, put the gin bottle, the tonic, and some glasses at a strategic position in the dining room, and set to. I tackled Ess's papers, preserving bundles of bills for Boomer, bundles of Bureau papers for Lois, and a bundle of personal odds and ends. Evie and Beeb took their gins with them, and started their investigation of Ess's clothes. We rendezvoused after forty minutes or so for another gin, and thereafter the sounds from upstairs suggested a lightening of spirits. After a second rendezvous, I was forced to abandon my role as paper-sorter, and had to act as arbiter in matters of taste. First Evie, then Evie and Beeb together, came down arrayed in garments of Ess's — shoes, dresses and in the end undergarments as well — asking me to gauge their suitability. By the time the pubs were open, the mood was one of carnival.

Evie, who I suspect has a certain amount of unallocated libido at her disposal, deemed that it was time we bundled what we didn't want for the Oxfam lady, and I took them both to lunch. All remaining papers I pitched into a sack for disposal, sight unseen, and the task was done. Beeb and Evie tottered over to the pub dressed entirely in Ess's garments. Even in her shoes. Bulging out of them, Beeb especially, they contrived to make clothes that had looked sober on Ess seem positively Bacchanalian. It's rare for a man of my years to play Silenus on a superb summer's day in the midst of a London suburb. But Evie and Beeb did me proud. By the time we'd wandered back to lie in the sun in Boomer's back garden, we were all very tight indeed.

The saloon bar is one of the great testing grounds : it's there, especially on a summer lunchtime, when you're tipsy, that you discover whether an attractive woman is a person of ethical worth. It's a moment when she's licensed to behave as though she's available : however surreptitiously, to hint that the man she's with could prove surplus to requirements. Though I had no claim on either, and we were tipsy enough to excuse marginal lapses of taste, they acquitted themselves perfectly. I was button-holed into a conversation of a ritualistic nature about the fuel consumptions of British and Japanese cars ; one that I quite enjoyed. Beeb and Evie entered with enthusiasm, meanwhile, on to the topic of azaleas. Their group swelled until it eventually numbered almost a dozen men, their womenfolk following them so as not to strain the leash. But they parried all intrusive remarks, allowing them to roll away in a harmless trail of rabbit droppings. Preserving their own self-respect and mine, snubbing no one, they passed the Saloon Bar Test with colours flying.

While we lay stuporous in Boomer's back garden, Evie, surprisingly wistfully, raised the question of Penny and Boomer :

'Beeb says she's knocking him about already.' And then, a while later, 'If she's not careful, she'll end up with the halt and lame like me ... You're expected to sit up half the night consoling them. You get so *weary* ... ' Consoling them, the television executives with artistic leanings who prey on her good nature while she pursues her slap-dash career around the fringe of their profession. She's sure that Penny and Boomer will burn their affair through in a month and end up hating each other ; and she wants to know why Boomer hasn't taken an interest in Persephone. It would suit them both : Persephone would not have to hang round Jimmy and Beeb, and Boomer could avoid a gratuitous mangling.

Boomer and Persephone? It's plausible. Boomer and Evie, come to that ; why not? That's plausible too. Wistfulness strikes a note adjacent to promise. But whether Boomer could stomach all those thrustful media men and second-rate actors I doubt.

Lounging there, under Boomer's locust tree, we were assuming, the three of us, that love's more like the opening of a trapdoor on obsession than mutual symbiotic melting. What we foresaw was a ravaging. Accordingly, it was in the spirit of visiting the sick that we decided to drop round on Penny and cadge tea.

Granted our prognostications, she cut an incongruous figure on her doorstep to greet us. She'd caught the sun, and beads of sweat stood out on her upper lip and brow. Far from ill, she brought to mind that old saw about the lineaments of gratified desire. Walking out into the garden, Evie slipped her arm through mine, and muttered in my ear : 'Christ, it's good while it lasts. You forget don't you ... ' But it doesn't last, the echo went. There are shadows across Evie's disposition to which Beeb seems immune.

Boomer was tending Perce's tomatoes, and emerged

cheerful from Perce's conservatory, thanking Beeb and Evie profusely for coping with Ess's belongings. Both had had the tact to take some of their acquisitions off before leaving, though Beeb, I noticed, had retained Ess's blouse. Penny had noticed too. But with Beeb inside it, the blouse was emblematic of a new order, in which dark thoughts of grave-robbing were out of place.

We cadged our tea, but felt like gate-crashers, and soon decamped. Beeb still thinks it could all turn out for the best, but Evie's sceptical; and although I've never seen Penny look so smashing, I'm afraid she's right. Superficially the signs are good, but ominous ones are visible too. Significantly, Penny's retinue of love-hungry men has begun to reassemble itself; and so too have her habitual methods of coping with it. These woebegones are a stick she used to beat Perce with; and I'd idly assumed that, now, they'd fade away. That she'd have no further use for them. But on today's showing, the habit is deeply engrained and its grip on her frighteningly mechanical.

During tea, she spent twenty minutes on the telephone. I saw her through the window, gesticulating with her free hand, listening to the incoming messages with an exaggerated expression of sympathy. It seemed that Jack was going to drop round; he needed to talk.

To the best of my recollection, Jack is the forward-looking urban studies teacher at the local comprehensive. Whether he likes it or not, Boomer is doomed to an evening in which Penny will listen with rapt attention to Jack's account of his conflict with his head teacher about who is to teach what to whom. Jack's emotions flow though a tap that Penny can twiddle at will. Patently he's a pain in the neck; and what she manages to suck from her sessions with him, I can only guess. His hot stares seem to nourish in her some deep-seated appetite for emotional vulgarity. It's wretches like Jack whom Penny occasionally lures into a sexual embrace, feeding in them God knows what fantasies of the carnal and compassionate realms at last conjoined. And it's wretches like him whom she then abandons in a steaming heap.

The retinue is going to reform itself with a vengeance now. Attractive widows of forty attract. And attractive widows of forty who glow as Penny now glows, do so fearsomely. There's Jack. There'll be Perce's boss, just ringing up to make sure that everything is OK. There'll be Perce's young henchman, fresh from the LSE, with what he hopes are black and lustrous eyes. There'll be Jack's friend who's impotent; and Jack's friend's friend, who can't make up his mind whether he's queer. The man from the local poetry reading society. The optician who runs the local amateur dramatic society and whose wife has just passed on. And his son, just going up to study something at Warwick. Lord, yes, and the bloke who repaired the conservatory last year, and who's really an out-of-work vet; and his friend who plays rugger for Rosslyn Park. The supply's unending. It's roughly the male population of the South-East. All will be treated with the same earnest concern, and all are potential debris.

I'm not sure how Boomer will cope, but he'll find it alien without a doubt. My guess is that he'll suffer wild pangs of jealousy; and if he does, that Penny will lead him a very uncomfortable dance indeed.

July 16th

A small item of wisdom, gathered from the back of a

matchbox. Among moles, the male tunnels in a straight line; the female tunnels in a curve. All the mysteries of sex and gender lie here explained!

July 30th

A fortnight's brutalising figure work. The first person I rang on emerging from this labyrinth of numbers into the light of day was Jimmy. He told me in passing that Boomer had been round: he was off somewhere to do a couple of lectures and to laze by the sea. Elsinor, Jimmy thought. And Penny hadn't gone with him. The atmosphere there was clouded, and Boomer on edge.

I rang Penny but she wasn't in — neither then nor later. I can picture her in the local, listening to Jack, laying her hand on his arm from time to time, even holding his hand. Or Mike. Or Geoff. And I can see Boomer at his conference, wherever it is, bathing his bruises in the briny.

Depressed, I rang Evie. She was gloomy too; she's saddled herself with another producer. But we had a cheery evening of it all the same: we saw an old Chabrol together and watched Stephane Audran. There was a half-seduction: Audran undressing a girl I didn't much like called 'Why'. It left me all aglow. What effect it had on Evie, I'm unsure, and don't feel I know her well enough to ask.

Afterwards, she told me a bit about her mogul, who whines about his wife whom he hasn't the least intention of leaving, and about his latent artistic talents that he wouldn't dream of putting to use. Being married isn't simple, I'm sure. But there are drawbacks to being unmarried, too. Sooner or later those whined-about spouses arrive on our doorsteps, granting us as they do so about as much sentience as the door-knob. However you view it, the terrain can look bleak.

I passed the thought on to Evie and suggested that she and I ought to found a self-protective co-operative. She thought that that was *exactly* what we should do — although, in spite of everything, she still wants to marry again. She can't see why, and neither can I, but she does. I told her she'd be very nice to be married to; and she warned me that she might hold me to it yet. She keeps hoping against hope that it isn't too late, and that she'll find someone to send her head over heels just once more. Penny's in the same boat, she thinks.

I asked for news, but she's heard nothing. Only that Jimmy and Beeb had gone round for a drink, and had had to put up with one of Penny's lame-ducks: some be-nighted soul whom Penny treated as if he were Che Guevara. I described Jack, but this one was younger and nastier. Boomer had been doing his best to look unper-turbed, but was hating it.

Evie pressed me about Penny, and her need to knock men about. Is it something she plans, or does she just find that she's doing it? Forced to guess, I said that probably she did think about it from time to time, but not hard enough to stop her doing it again. I've noticed that if she's driven to do something, Penny always seems to find that something naturally just. Boomer might shake her out of it, but I don't fancy his chances. She can play on his jealousy, and she can play on his *amour propre*, too. The competition she'll trail before him won't be of his peers; men he can find some way of respecting as a refuge from his wretchedness. They'll be creeps. And their very inferiority will be Penny's trump card. The way to break a man like Boomer down is to lavish attention on someone he sees as beneath contempt. Penny'll know that by instinct; and the taller the rock-pile of pride, the easier the attack on it becomes.

We got back to Highgate at about eleven, and went in to see Jimmy and Beeb. They'd guests. A young man I didn't know. A slightly less young man I thought I recognised but couldn't place. And Persephone. Some of them, perhaps all of them, had been to the Roundhouse, and were chatting about it in a desultory way.

Having helped push the Roundhouse production around for a while, Evie announced our anti-marriage co-operative. Beeb enlisted at once, and Jimmy seemed to think it a good scheme. I expected Persephone to join, but she kept quiet. Instead, the young man I didn't know pointed out that the co-operative would itself become a form of marriage, and soon enough its members would go round grumbling and whining about one another like everyone else. It was cleverly put. Evie reproved him for being worldly-wise and he blushed, which made him seem more pleasant. In the midst of this, Evie's new mogul rang, and she trudged over to the phone. I could hear her explaining that she'd gone to the flicks with an old friend. She had then to explain that I *was* male, but the spirit was one of probity, and 'Oh, no, for Christ's sake! It wasn't that sort of thing at all ... '

She came back tired. Flopping down next to me, she said she meant it, and let's set up shop before she drowned in the squalor of it all, and lost the will. And then after a moody pause, she looked at me as if the thought had struck her seriously for the first time: 'C'mon, it wouldn't be bad, would it?' She might have been her father contemplating the purchase of an outlying farm. I felt like rolling acres and fox coverts, the occasional wood or two. It sounded a pleasant enough arrangement, and I was on the point of saying so when I found Persephone watching us attentively. We were offering ourselves to the younger generation as travel-stained and tatty, when, for my money, there was something more ambitious to be said. It was this more ambitious something, I surmised, that young Persephone was listening for.

Without premeditation, I embarked on a panegyric in favour of the Mystic Search. The pursuit of the luminous wonder that flits through our lives in unpredictable ways, elusively, and lends a sense of purpose to processes that would otherwise amount to sordid mantlings together of nuts and bolts. I spoke with fervour of that girl on the flight to Düsseldorf, with her violin case, and with whom I plucked up courage to exchange not a syllable. And that other girl walking down Dundas Street, the sun pouring through her hair, an aureolin smudge against blackened Edinburgh stone, and gone before I could take her in. I touched on Stephane Audran and Ess too.

It went on for several minutes and was in my best oratorical style. In fact, it was the best speech of my life : my moment of eloquence. In the course of it, I paid special attention to the quality of reticence ; the sense of poise and distance that makes it possible to believe in sex, however fleetingly, as the gateway to the mind. Not the bread and potatoes of personal attraction, but fascination with the idea of an intimacy that could prove aesthetically sound. In any heterosexual bachelor's biography, there are amorous episodes : ladies who offer themselves under various rubrics, some with prefatory romance, some without. Bodies you get used to, with more or less pleasure. But in none of these more humdrum expressions of the genre is there evidence of the body as an object that the mind can irradiate. The women of my Pantheon belong to another frame of reference altogether.

When it was over, Evie, Beeb and Jimmy were delighted with me. They applauded, and both Evie and Beeb kissed me, Beeb moist-eyed. Jimmy said he specially loved the bits about nuts and bolts and glistening tresses : and how right I was. There's a trick of nature whereby the merest outline of a beautiful lower limb, the contour of a face, can awaken in us the belief that the woman before us is a creature of exquisite discrimination. The spectacle of a beautiful body creates the illusion of a beautiful mind ; and it's this hallucinatory echo that makes living with one another possible, enabling us to survive the extraordinary ambiguities of sex, not just for a week or two, while we're buoyed up by novelty, but year after year. By rights, it's a recipe for endless disillusionment : the discovery, time and again, that beautiful bodies house minds of deepest banality. But once we've learnt a little wisdom, and are not too specific, it's a trick that'll last us a lifetime. You live on the memory of a glance ; we all do. He was parodying himself, placing us in inverted commas, and providing just the sense of distance that images of resplendent tresses and fetching severity deserve. But he was moved too ; just a little, at least. And while we talked he'd put his hand unselfconsciously on Beeb's apricot-coloured knee. It's the first time I've seen him touch her ; and an insight of a sort into the workings of his curious psyche.

The younger generation, on the other hand, were looking uneasy : simply puzzled in Persephone's case ; actively embarrassed in the case of the two young men. Theirs is a whole different scene. The other young man, the one I thought I recognised, decided that it was time he contributed. Enough's enough. It was time we were all wrenched back to the realities of the dialectic. He couldn't manage the irony, though, making himself seem what I suddenly remembered he was : a university demagogue of the new and humourless school. Once an insurgent ; now lecturer in sociology and minor television star.

Jimmy, Beeb, Evie and I subsided with a collective, almost silent Oh-my-God, and our mood of revival evaporated. But Persephone came to our rescue. Having been quiet, she silenced the young man from the barricades : her 'Use your wits' was spoken in a tone to suggest that hers was the last family left alive in London with a nanny. Unused to such treatment, he was half-way into his first sentence of self-justification when she flagged him down : 'You're out of your depth. Just listen.'

A young woman of forceful character. He was drawing breath to start again along the path that leads all good men to Hegel, when she gave him a further warning glance, and to my relief he held back. In the manner of his generation, he must be in love ; and a remarkable figure he cut there, in the middle of Beeb's carpet. Persephone seemed immune to his charm, however. I had the flattering sense that, between us, Jimmy and I had struck sparks that she wanted to watch all the way to the floor. The patter about Hegel she could take as read. Likewise the patterer.

July 31st

Last night was comforting. There was a snag, though,

that I've been slow to remember. Jimmy had something else to say about those idealising glimpses: a loose-end with ominous implications. The ideal inspires hope, but at the same time kindles the urge to *know*. And the urge for knowledge is bifurcated, fork-tongued. There's factual knowledge and there's also carnal knowledge. And not just bifurcated but treacherous. The worm in the rose. For the more we know, the harder we find it to keep our sustaining vision of the known intact.

I wonder what Beeb made of that. What I make of it, come to that. She seemed unruffled, so presumably he spoke from their shared wisdom rather than off his own bat. She was unruffled, too, the night she dropped a depth-charge in the midst of Jimmy's last birthday party. He was reinventing as usual: domestic machinery and its place in our imaginations, and how sad it is that the vulgar Würlitzer eroticism of the early fridges has given way to white cubes.

We'd got ourselves stuck somewhere between *Architectural Review* and *Which?* and were getting bored with ourselves. Having sat silent, staring out of the window, Beeb announced that all the more earth-shattering of her own erotic experiences occurred while she was spread-eagled over her tumble dryer. Hundreds of thousands of women must have made the same discovery; so why not celebrate it in a new style, moulded to the shape of the body like Italian sculpture. Even upholstered.

Unlike the rest of us, Beeb doesn't speak for effect. The thought struck her, and she passed it on. It was as simple as that. Jimmy tried to maintain his Treasury sang-froid, but blushed scarlet, as well he might. I was startled, almost out of my wits. And Penny was shocked. What offended her, I'm almost sure, was Beeb's manner. If she'd put her proposition across as an attempt to be wild or outrageous, Penny would have blenched, but taken it in good part. But expressed candidly, it disgusted her. It's just occurred to me that she might have been knocking Boomer about so severely because he's candid too: perhaps any expression of appetite that's undisguised sets up in her an undertow of distaste.

August 1st

I must pluck up courage to ask Evie why her marriage to Jimmy didn't work. She's reticent about such matters. Rather, it's she who decides whether she is going to be reticent about such matters or not.

All Penny can tell me is that when Evie and Jimmy split up, instead of setting up separate establishments, they simply divided their house. Upstairs, Mr Right moved in with Evie, while downstairs Jimmy set up home with Beeb. Evie got bored with Mr Right and pitched him out; but meanwhile had had Nicky and Peter. Now Beeb and Jimmy bring up Nicky and Peter, and Evie is a working woman. It's always struck me as odd that with sisters so alike, both glamorous and sophisticated girls, Jimmy should live so happily with one, having failed to live happily with the other. You'd expect him to choose someone quite unlike Evie. Her opposite, even. But I've felt all along that it's their very similarity that does the trick: a man with the need to live with the same person under two dispensations, as husband and lover. To be married and not married at the same time. What convoluted souls our administrative wizards are!

August 2nd

At last, I've spoken to Penny about cash. Pa has promised to cover the girls' school fees, and there's enough in the Nat West to tide her over for the time being. She's going to sell the house and find something smaller. And so is Boomer. She spoke as if her finances and Boomer's might become inseparably linked; even as if some arrangement's already been reached. She's in good form, but her tone jars. It's as if she's committed herself to Boomer, but is going to squeeze him down into a Perce-shaped lump before she'll marry him. She's compelled to marry, but can only tolerate a husband who'll behave as if he's Perce. I want to tell her that Perces are born not made; not, anyway, in middle-age and from material as unlikely as Boomer. Squeeze him down to shape and size, and what she'll have in her hands is not a leathery entity like Perce, but a juiceless lump. That's not a speech for Penny's kitchen, though, with Boomer pacing round the rest of the ground floor, picking things up and putting them down, as if there's something he needs to say, but which keeps contorting itself hopelessly into knots. I'm not convinced, in any case, that she has the strength in her wrists to do the squeezing.

Sometime this week, I'll go and have a word with Young Eric, and find out whether Perce was properly insured.

August 6th

Visit your family accountant, and find every secret revealed! Each time I visit Eric, I'm persuaded that he

117

ought to have been a theatrical agent and not an accountant at all. Not for nothing does he boast that he can transact any item of business under the sun, as long as it takes less than three minutes.

After a moment's condolence, we settled into what he observed was an improper conversation about Perce's finances. Completing a few summarising remarks about Perce's life policies, he swept, in best Show Biz style, into the opening that I'd inadvertently provided.

I knew, of course, about the Sunnymead Trust? I didn't. Nor does Penny. Delighted, Eric then led me through into a side of Perce's life I'd no inkling of. The story centres on a shadowy figure called Farquhar-Fore, now domiciled in Tenerife. Farquhar-Fore, whom Eric has only met once, had worked in the same office as Perce; a motivational psychologist, late of Oxford University. In Eric's judgment, no fool, he'd realised that scholarship and good intentions were not enough. They must be set to use.

Did I know that there was a social migration afoot in our society, apropos the mentally ill? That our mental hospitals have been exporting their inmates, sending them back to the communities whence they came? As it happens, I had. In the course of my somewhat one-sided romance with Beth, she printed on my mind her belief that we must break down the madhouse walls, and set patients free to make normal lives for themselves. A second item of her doctrine was that people don't just go mad, they're driven mad by their parents. It bothered me at the time that these two attractive-seeming beliefs should mesh together so poorly. For if long-stay patients are sent out into the community, where can they go but to the very relatives who drove them barmy in the first place?

When I aired this inconsistency, she was lividly angry; angry enough to leave me on the verge of panic. And faced with such an onslaught, I happily forsook logic and settled for her goodwill and wonderful food. But the same discrepancy had struck Farquhar-Fore; and he had been free to press the analysis home. He saw that the defective and mad were being turned loose in large numbers: because it was enlightened to do so, and cheap. Also, that their relatives would be ashamed of them. Or dispersed. Or dead. And that they would be left on the parish. But he also twigged that with the Costa Brava boom, our South Coast boarding houses would be losing trade, and in any case, stand empty for much of the year. Why not press them into service as permanent seaside homes for the mad? Per capita, per week, income would be small. But dozens could be packed into small buildings all the year round, and standards of catering could be low. For an organisation that had as its head a man with a doctorate in psychology from an ancient university, and as business manager an executive of proven commercial experience, the potential profit was immense.

Hence Farquhar-Fore and Perce. Hence the Sunnymead Trust. And Farquhar-Fore had been right; it *was* a gold mine. They had started with a single boarding house in Broadstairs. The next year, they could buy three more. Then another five, scattered along the coasts of Sussex and Kent. In each, they installed a landlady to dispense food and pills; and packed in their loonies, five to a bedroom, and stacked in rows around the television set in the lounge. Farquhar-Fore was on hand as director, while Perce saw to the collection of the rent.

On paper, a humane and intellectually respectable solution to an intractable social problem. In reality, a five-star ramp. Initially, the two of them ran the trust from their office as a side line. But local health authority officials and hospital superintendents loved them, and soon enough Farquhar-Fore moved out, and conducted his share of the enterprise from his flat. Yet as soon as the money began to flow, Perce committed his blunder. He insisted on a fixed salary from the trust, rather than a percentage. Eric mentioned the figure of £6,000 a year, what was left going to Farquhar-Fore. In the first two years, Perce did well. But in the third, fourth and fifth years, income soared and trendy young Farquhar-Fore was suddenly rich, trendy young Farquhar-Fore; a man with a tax problem, and a controlling interest in a wonderful white hotel.

Young Eric votes Labour and lives in Canonbury, and he views Perce's exploit with shocked distaste. But what really hurt was the mindlessness of Perce's caution. He warned Perce sternly; and on one occasion harangued him. But Perce would not budge. The prospect of living the life of the blithe, disporting himself with brown-limbed young widows in the Bahamas, moved him not a jot. He was pleased to be canny while Farquhar-Fore frolicked. To emphasise his distress, Eric paced his office, giving me a replay of his efforts to cajole Perce towards the twin paths of Fun and Mammon, throwing in for good measure an imitation of Perce's rearguard against blandishment almost as cruel as Penny's.

How big is Penny's share of Sunnymead? Eric doesn't know. Arguably, she has half the freehold of a string of seedy seaside boarding houses; arguably she doesn't. It's a matter of interpretation. Farquhar-Fore might settle for a quiet life, and buy her out; but if he doesn't, costs will mount.

Eric, in any case, was in no mood to dwell on the prosaic. He wanted to capture something for my edification about what had made Perce tick. Perce *had* managed to pull a fast one after all; albeit, cautiously. Just adventurous enough, he'd fallen in with a scheme that most of his business colleagues would have dismissed as harebrained. But the moment he sensed the golden glow of real money, he'd backed off. The prospect of loot had set his nerves a-jangle. The god that rules Perce's slice of the firmament deems that profit without commensurate suffering is a sin. And although his loonies had doubtless suffered — more, probably, than they had in their wards — for Perce it had all been alarmingly effortless.

It makes perfect sense that he should have kept Sunnymead hidden from Penny. She would have plagued him out of his wits about it. But what about Ess? He could well have confided in her, and have been taking her down to inspect part of the Sunnymead empire on the day of the crash.

When I told Penny about Sunnymead this evening, she was obviously stung; but all she would commit herself to was something contemptuous about 'Sunnymead' as a choice of name. I tried to interest her in the money that might be coming her way, but she took not the slightest notice. If I'd heard about it all a month ago, I would have gone down to the coast to take a look for myself. I might even have written to Farquhar-Fore. But by now the ashes are cooling, and I'm losing the urge to stir them.

August 7th

Normally my sister's improvidence irritates me, but this

morning I woke feeling sorry for her; and decided to go back in search of the necklace I saw last week in Chalk Farm. And there it was: the kind of object to deny everything the Farquhar-Fores stand for. A series of yellowish lumps, irregular and large: copal amber, probably from Mali, spaced out with old elephant ivory and ultramarine glass. The whole thing's filthy, and looped together on an evil-smelling leather thong.

Very moving, I find it. The thought of those globules dripping from trees all those eons ago, fossilising in African mud. Their energy, and the black necks they've adorned for a century or more. Even the association with copal varnish, and the way painters have used it to protect their fleshy swathes of pigment.

When I got down to Penny's this evening, the scene was almost an exact replica of my last sight of it: Penny cheerful, Boomer agitated. I gave Penny her beads. She held them up and said how lovely, and kissed me for them, but put them on the kitchen dresser and made no attempt to wear them. She's no idea they cost me half a week's salary, and are special. In fact, she doesn't seem to like them. They fall into some category of hers like 'African Tat'; and as far as she's concerned, that's that. I feel quite irrationally cast down — which is silly, because if you'd asked me this morning to say dispassionately whether I thought she'd like them, I would have said probably not.

I didn't have long to wait to discover what was upsetting Boomer. Penny threw him her purse and sent us round to the pub for some beer. 'Rodge' was coming. He told me that Rodge was loathsome, but that he could not get Penny to see that. I bet he can't. It's precisely Rodge's loathsomeness she's using to knock Boomer into the shape she needs.

Penny was on the phone for a while. No Jack, it wasn't a good moment to pop round. What about tomorrow sometime? How bloody for you. But no. Tonight was no good. What about tomorrow? Oh, her brother had come down to talk about money. It would have to be tomorrow.

At this juncture, a sickly-looking young person of indeterminate gender wandered into the room and slumped into a chair. An acquaintance of my nieces I assumed; one whom Penny ought to discourage. Definitely masculine on closer scrutiny, the representative of the new order lit a cigarette and flipped idly through a magazine while we waited. As far as I could detect, he gave neither Boomer nor myself the slightest inflection of recognition.

When Penny eventually joined us, she exclaimed 'Rodge!' in her best good-trouper tones, and instructed Boomer to give him a beer. Boomer stood like a tired circus horse to do as he was bid. He poured out the beer into a glass, and handed it to the youth, who's rather older than I first thought. He then trudged back to his chair on the other side of the room. The youth had not looked at him; just reached out a hand. Penny announced superfluously that it had been Jack on the phone, but making her point none the less. She'd told him not to come round, but he might all the same.

Then, turning full-beam on Rodge, she wanted to know how it was all going. In the course of the next forty-five minutes, it transpired that Rodge's problem is a grant to do postgraduate research. Rodge is undecided, still, whether to take it up, or whether to go to Ibiza instead. In the course of this exposition, he used the first person singular more often than I would have believed syntactically possible. Beyond that, he seems to know best the expressions 'hassle', 'no way', and 'rip off'. The universities,

for example, are the first and third of these. 'Embarrassin''
is another weapon in Rodge's semantic armoury: an
adjective used to dismiss most of the suggestions Penny
fed him.

Almost at once, it was clear that Penny was hooked:
desperately keen that he should keep up his studies and
that he should not go to Ibiza. Equally, it was clear that
going-to-Ibiza was the lever with which Rodge brought
her back into line whenever she showed signs of wavering
in her devotion to his predicament. She sat on the floor,
cross-legged, while he milked her dextrously of sympathy,
glancing this way and that, but never for a moment looking one of us in the eye. Rather more slowly, it dawned
on me that, in his own brand of infighting, Rodge was
quite formidable. She kept urging him to take his research seriously, while he played hide-and-seek, finding
it all embarrassin', and hinting that he was on the point
of abandoning the whole hassle.

The research for which he has been given a grant is
predictably à la mode: something to do with the Frankfurt
School and their philosophical doctrines, a system of
thought I'm fairly sure he has misunderstood. Both Penny
and Rodge took it for granted that neither Boomer nor I
had anything pertinent to contribute. Boomer did intervene at one point, when Rodge had been more than
usually specious, but was shushed into silence by Penny
for his pains. We were enlisted, though, when it came to
the hassles attendant on registration and admission. Rodge
is convinced that the university functionaries have turned
against him, but Penny hurried in with her reassurances.
Boomer and I would see to that: I who have the most
tenuous contact with my own university, and Boomer who
has no contact with a university at all.

Bewildered, Boomer and I finally made off into the kitchen. In her bid to save Rodge's talent for posterity, rather than let it dissipate itself in Ibiza, Penny did not appear to notice us go. Out in the kitchen, Boomer and I settled down, waiting for the siege to end. From next door, there came the sounds of Penny's cajoling : mostly serious, but interlaced with moments more flirtatiously gay. A hammed performance of Ageing Trendy, a role I know her to despise.

Boomer explained a little to me. Rodge had somehow engineered for himself a barbiturate addiction, and was also launched on a career of living off unhappy, middle-aged women. He is now cured, but can presumably slip back in the winking of a bloodless eye. Ibiza is the home of his addiction, and also that of a more than usually importunate young matron. Hence Penny's zeal for the scholarly life, and the curious nature of his hold. At every step, he can slip back into his bad old ways ; and the burden of persuasion lies entirely with her. Boomer waved his hands in the air as he described this, aghast that Penny, *his* Penny, could not see the vulgarity of her plight. Normally so quick, she's fallen for the cheapest trick in the textbook : 'Look-what-you're-making-me-do'. She's jealous. She's allowed herself to believe that it'll be her fault and failing if he goes back to his pills. And, incredibly, it seems that she may even be excited at the thought of taking this doubtful Abelard to her breast, and thereby giving him back the will to work. And when Boomer suggested that she heave him out, he'd been told that her feelings towards Rodge were motherly, and that his own doubts were ridiculous.

Miserably, Boomer pushed breadcrumbs around on the kitchen table's surface, and had nothing more to add. In the end, we went round to the pub. Getting back a little before ten, we found Rodge still installed: I heard the word 'embarrassin'' floating on the air as I went past the sitting room door. Also Jack; he must have gate-crashed after all.

Poor Penny. The biter bit. At a low ebb, she's met her match. And Rodge is better equipped to fight her to a stalemate than Boomer ever was. He has nothing to lose. He can go back to his pills, or pretend to. He can take up with his biddy in Ibiza, and abandon his academic career. And he can let Penny know that he talks about her behind her back as one of the old ladies he's shafted. Press him really hard, and he can commit suicide. Like Waterloo, it's going to be a damn close-run thing.

August 19th

Another spell in the labyrinth. From time to time I surface, but am so dazed that I can think of nothing to do but plunge back in.

August 21st

A lugubrious evening with Boomer in front of the television. The episode with Penny's obviously almost over, and its cauterising effect nearly complete. He mentioned Ess, and there was that hint of eulogy again in what he had to say. From time to time, he said, she gave you a chance to see her inner life. Was it sleight-of-hand? — he wasn't sure. The phrase brought back her Dad and his conjuring shows. If Ess's was a species of conjuring, she'd certainly practised it in some unusually interesting times and places. I said as much to Boomer, but he seemed not to hear.

Our vital energies depleted, we settled to watch recorded highlights of the Davis Cup on the telly. Someone (Beatrice Webb?) said that marriage is the waste basket of the emotions. Nonsense. The great waste basket is sport. When down at the mouth, creatures like Jimmy, Boomer and myself are prepared to chart our every existential twitch and node in terms of the recorded highlights of this and that.

In spite of myself, I noticed that the rather elderly sounding commentator was someone I'd been murdered by at squash when we were both at school; and his 'discussant' a man, now retired, whom I'd first watched in the flesh when he was a local prodigy of twelve. I tried to interest Boomer in the ironies of the scene flickering around in front of us, but he was in no mood for them, so we relapsed into silent watching. Before we went to bed, we had a little therapeutic whisky, and without warning he plunged off once again into sporting autobiography.

His contention is that when he was young, he was small and cowardly. His head balanced on a long thin neck, and his shoulder blades stood out like wings. For eighteen months or so, when nine or ten, he'd been bullied on his way home from school each day by two slightly older boys. Hogg, one was called, and the other something like Bastin. They didn't knock him around, but were clever enough to carry him all the while along the knife-edge of doubt, probing his sense of fear and impotence in cruel and clever ways.

In the end, they went to different schools, or at least on different buses, and the persecution was over. Meanwhile Boomer grew and grew. At seventeen, he'd become one of those over-muscled young toughs who churn up and down suburban swimming pools, emptying the water out into the surrounding cubicles. He played water polo for a club, and as a crawl swimmer was caught at a threshold between being quick and being very quick; between thrashing up and down, and slipping through the chlorinated water like a silken thread.

It all boiled down to a pause in his stroke as he turned his head to breathe. It was the legacy of learning to swim late because of the war, and he could never quite eradicate it. Anyway, one morning Boomer was standing at the end of the pool, waiting to get started, when he saw, coming towards him, a nervous, short-sighted figure; head held up to keep the water away from his face, executing a feeble breaststroke. Closer, and Boomer realised that it was the execrable Hogg, now half-way down the bath, and half-way along his trajectory from primary-school sadist to family solicitor. Boomer knew with certainty that it was within his power to drown him. Metaphorically; and also, if he chose, literally. He could dive in on top of him, and repay years of humiliation with a few seconds of unalloyed terror.

The figure moved closer and closer to what infantry officers call the killing zone, and Boomer poised waiting. Telling the story, Boomer says that he experienced in those few moments everything that there was to experience about the baths, and the curiously lower-middle-class life they contained: the Edwardian white tiling; the slight haze of steam that hung over the water's surface; the rim of Brylcreem that collected around the water's edge; the exact note on which his coach, a local policeman, intoned the rhythm of the crawl swimmer's breathing —

'In-aile … Ex-aile … In-aile … Ex-aile … ' Even the huge mirror at the end of the pool in which the youth of the town arranged the oily quiffs in their hair before emerging into the High Street ; and in which Boomer had recently caught sight of himself in a body that he didn't immediately recognise as his own — a structure of lumps and bulges borrowed from the body-building magazines, rather than the bird-like set of bones he felt at home in.

But poor Boomer, despite those acres of rippling muscle, did nothing. He was transfixed. Instead of landing like Genghis Khan all over the hapless Hogg, still sneering at the world but now a potential loser, Boomer watched him while he made his way right through the killing zone, and allowed him to reach anchor almost at his feet, close enough to touch. Only then did Boomer dive in and swim away.

The thematic congruence of this tale with his one about the *Scharnhorst* was strong. And hearing him tell what was in effect the same story twice, either side of his relationship with Penny, once before and once after, it occurred that Boomer must have retold it dozens of times in the course of the last twenty years or so, when feeling bleak. And he will have told it in the hope of finding an echo in his audience ; and through that echo, some sort of resolution. And each time, the human race will have failed him, feeding him responses from the great liberal bran bag about how it wasn't cowardice at all, and about how unevolved it would have been to aggress the Hogg in that way.

Unfortunately, it embarrasses me to hear the same story twice, even if it has been transposed. So I took refuge behind the thought that the pregnant moments in our lives are often those in which nothing happens. (And that as a consequence, the novel of action is a special kind of fraud.)

August 22nd

It's sweltering. And high time that I went to see the Voisins.

August 23rd

A call from Boomer. He's got a God-sent invitation to go to the States for a year, and is taking it. He sounded deathly tired, but not rubble.

I am fairly sure that the moment Penny discovers this, she'll lose all interest in Jack's problems, or in saving Rodge's soul for scholarship. Her fascination with them is ancillary to the primary relationship in her life : with Boomer, and before him with Perce. Take the primary away, and the secondary evaporates.

August 25th

On the Highgate tube this morning, it was hotter than any English conveyance has a right to be. More like a hijacking than a commuter run. To my left, clutching the same overhead bar as myself, was a girl of nineteen or twenty ; predominantly Indian, but with a splash of something else — Levantine maybe, or Jewish. Childishly slim, but with breasts disproportionately large ; nipples forward-facing, in the way of which I privately disapprove. The headlamp look. She was dressed all in white ; jeans so tight that they must have hurt, and a flimsy tee shirt.

Justified by the heat, she was bra-less; the shape of her nipples being obvious in every detail through the white cotton. Frizzy hair, eyes black; a Persian painting's eyes. And the pout of a mouth that Ronald Searle puts on his barmaids. Clutching there, her hand was surprisingly large, like her breasts; simian almost, sprouting from a small wrist. A gibbon's hand. The nails unmanicured and, on two quicks, the rudiments of what'll become painful hang-nails. Her little finger had a largish lump of turquoise set in silver, and her second finger a topaz in rough gold. The watch strap around her child's wrist was well-used and massively masculine. Between bouts of staring into space, she was reading a paperback over the shoulder of the young man half between us: *The Longest Journey* — in the circumstances, apposite enough.

Not my type; but beyond the occasional fingers of cool air wafting in to us via the carriage window, I could find nothing in the world to concentrate my mind on besides her physical presence. The young man with the paperback was having the same trouble, I'm almost sure.

As we left Camden Town and set off towards Euston, the train lurched viciously, throwing me forward on top of two small boys in school uniform, lodged between my brief case and the bottom of a middle-aged woman who looked as if she might be a librarian, but for all I knew is a Junior Cabinet Minister. All I could see of the boys was curly hair, and corners of tie and shirt. Having lurched us all forward, the train lurched us backwards, pressing me back on to the woman I'd detected behind me, and who I intuited was the small boys' mother.

In the next minute or so, the pressure down my back became firmer and firmer. Her breasts were pressed into my back, and her stomach against my bottom. With every-one else in that dangerous steel container, I'd taken off what I could, my jacket over my arm. We were pressed as close to each other as a married couple in bed.

That pressure on my back was ambiguous. She could have been pressing forward so as not to lose contact with her sons, still tucked in round the other side of me ; or simply to ensure that she was near enough to the doors to get free at the next stop. As Euston approached, and the train slowed, the disposition of the bodies around us shifted, and she was able to squeeze round my right shoulder, and make contact once more with her children. We stood side by side, sardine-style, for fifteen seconds or so. Rather stockily built, she was curly-headed like her sons ; neither dark nor blonde. She shops at Habitat, but is married to someone unadventurous ; a High Barnet surveyor.

As the train stopped, she looked my way for a moment, and said 'Sorry'. Then, gathering her sons with difficulty, she disappeared.

It could have been an embarrassed or falsely vivacious thing to say ; but what she conveyed was apology for implicating me, without invitation, in an aspect of her intimate life that was normally her own preserve. Impli-citly, she neither asserted nor denied that she'd pressed against me on purpose. Equally, she left open the question of whether she'd found the pressure privately exciting. A rare expression of candour. One that drowned out the Persian concubine entirely, and brought back to my mind, for no reason that I can immediately place, my dream of Ess in her mortuary drawer.

Odd how I never need to write when I'm with the Voisins. Now, when I'm back, yes. But at the time, no. France must exert a soothing influence.

Marguerite, I realise, is a woman who keeps an endogenous jitteriness at bay by undertaking more than any sane woman should. It's not just that the Paris school system needs administering; visiting males like myself need administering too. Didier and I get on happily listening in the other's language and answering in our own; but it's an *ad hoc* arrangement that plays on Marguerite's nerves. And it enrages her if I try to cope in this way with her kids. It's a source of scandal to her, too, that I'd a thousand times rather sit at home with them, reading the *Guide Verte*, than hurtle round the Normandy countryside, stopping to look at sights deemed to merit two stars or more.

This time, though, circumstances were stubbornly hostile to her. The kids were ill, one after the other, and had to be taken back, one after the other, all the way to Paris to be dosed by France's only competent paediatrician. The bedraggled Renault was ailing too. So in practice there was little she could do to stop me lounging on the beach, staring into the blue void.

First the Trouville beach, and then the Deauville beach. The twin nodes of Elysium. At Trouville you're surrounded by pony carts, and round the corner there's the house by the quay where Flaubert toyed in his imagination with *Madame Bovary*. Overhead, another pre-war touch, there trudge tiny monoplanes, towing advertisements. You're instructed to knit with a particular brand of wool, and to read the latest bestseller — *Bakchich* by a certain Michel Clerc. Lucky Michel Clerc.

But this year, a disconcerting novelty, too: huge graffiti adorn the brickwork of the Trouville Yacht Club. *'Gardez Votre Pudeur.'* Then, adjacent to this, in the same hand: *'Aujourdhui Mono Demain Prostitution No Toples Obben Ohne Nicht A La Reine Des Plages Familiales.'* It was not till I went across the bridge to Deauville that I saw what had upset the paint-brush wielder so. We'd been there on the Deauville sand, a family group among family groups, for half an a hour or so, when down among us there picked their way two young women. The older, in high-heeled espadrilles and a turban, stopped within two yards of us; and as she stood, took off all her clothes apart from her turban and the bottom half of a minimal bikini. Bright red tee-shirt with slashed sleeves; jeans; those preposterously tilted espadrilles — all these she shed, and then arranged herself on a small mat and began to sun-bathe. She was as near to me as if she'd been a member of our own circle who for some reason had moved a small distance away.

Looking around I saw that there were others. Here and there, among the mums and dads and toddlers, other young women were sunning themselves with their top halves exposed. At first, I couldn't make out whether I was supposed to look. Were we, grown-ups and children, supposed to take this half-naked woman in our midst for granted — to look through her or past her? Or were we allowed to stare? And if stare, how much appreciation could we display? My discovery was that while the Voisins were looking past or through, I'd been evolving stratagems whereby, hidden behind my dark glasses, I could legitimately glance around the beach, taking her in as I did so. A group of Germans playing ineptly with a volleyball were proving most helpful in this respect. Wandering dogs were useful too. I was constrained to be surreptitious though ; I was scared of meeting her eye.

The girl with her was not glamorous in the least ; I took her to be a younger sister. She was peeling badly, and was having trouble inflating a Lilo. They had a spaniel too : a breed with dirty habits, but in this case, pleasant enough. The sisters were taking it in turns to bury a stone for him, and, enthusiasm unflagging, he was digging it up.

The topless sister was married ; and also, as far as I could discern, physically perfect. Perfect in the rare sense that, while formally immaculate, she conveyed the impression of vulnerability. Monica Vitti on stilts. The body as envelope of the spirit.

The part of her nearest me, nine feet away, was her left breast and armpit, fittingly unshaved ; evidence that, however briefly, the ideal and corporeal sometimes coincide. What she brought to mind, beyond the great nudes in landscape, were images from natural history : saxifrage growing in shale, or the ripple-less dive of the grebe in search of fish. More pretentious still, the way in which bubbles rise to the surface of the best French mineral water : the Perrier this girl would always reject in favour of a Coke.

She had enough of a model girl's swagger to guarantee that she works somewhere in the world of professional beauty. With a body like hers, she could scarcely do anything else. Later in the afternoon, the beach photographer came over and they shook hands like business acquaintances. She made not the slightest attempt to cover her breasts the while.

But she's not made it yet. She's still offering herself far

135

and wide, and has yet to learn that gifts like hers are best hoarded. If she were already in the big time, she wouldn't be bothering to disport herself with such élan on Deauville beach.

A model or dancer, then. Somewhere local. Just possibly a stripper. Toplessness as she interprets it, though, is a species of art : a vehicle not just for finesse but a certain rustic gusto. At one stage, she ran down into the sea and splashed water over her breasts, clutching them as she ran — not out of prudery, she seemed to suggest, but because of their exceptional value. At another juncture, she stood, slipped her tee-shirt and espadrilles back on, and teetered off in search of an ice-cream. The effect was transfixing. She then allowed her sister to touch up her nail varnish for her, the reek of the lacquer wafting across the brief stretch of sand between her fingers and my nose. Later still, she got up and ran around a little for the spaniel, throwing a stick. She was relatively unathletic. Not compact or well-knit ; just a shade heavy in hip and breast, though otherwise slim. But even in this she succeeded in emphasising that her gifts were ultimately horizontal, not a matter of athletic capering in a public place. She'd be hopeless at tennis ; but so much the worse for tennis.

Towards the end of the afternoon, chatting in a quick undertone to her sister and making her giggle, she settled to knit. For this purpose, the tee-shirt went back on ; and freakishly orangey-pink wool worked its way with speed into the beginnings of a skimpy jumper. She was much more a peasant girl than I'd thought her at the beginning ; only recently up from somewhere half-buried near Clermont-Ferrand or Bordeaux, and keeping her sib in stitches about the ways of metropolitan men.

Observing furtively for the rest of my stay, I discovered that her approach to toplessness is unusual. Only one woman in fifty is taking the top of her costume off in Deauville this year, normally when lying down. Most are married women, accompanied either by husbands or young children. Those few unaccompanied are more likely to be in their forties, fifties or sixties than their teens. And of the young or youngish, this one of ours was the only one to behave as if her breasts were entities of intense significance, the focal centre of a civilisation. The others are reading from another script altogether. 'Children of nature', they're pretending they are free, and that their breasts are of no more interest than their knees or thumbs.

It still seems to me a pity that there should be so little connection between the vistas of sublimity that that girl's body opens up in the receptive male eye, and the professional world of tits and bums into which she presumably longs to break. I'll guarantee that I'd recognise that wonderful left breast of hers anywhere in the world : in any advertisement for a deodorant or bra. But what a waste. The comfort, if there is one, is that she'll fail to make it, and that the crowning performance of herself she'll give will be the one on the beach that the Voisins and I are privileged to have seen.

That evening, I plucked up courage to ask Marguerite about her, couching my inquiry in cautiously sociological terms, but she dismissed the topic with a 'pouf', as unworthy of a serious sentence. Afterwards, as I tried to get to sleep, listening with half my mind to the World Service, I realised to what an extent that girl had had the opportunity to smudge the boundaries of *mise en scène*. A venue normally dictates its own terms : a beach is a beach, a theatre is a theatre, a photographer's studio is a photographer's studio. To each venue, its own ground rules.

But Deauville beach is a place where venues melt a little, one into another. Where a beautiful girl is able to play all sorts of games along the boundary lines – reminding you of where you assume they lie, then uprooting you, causing a revitalising thrill as she does so. Like love, but less alarming. If boundaries were to dissolve entirely, and everything were possible everywhere, she'd be out of business. But that is Deauville's fascination : it retains its air of propriety, yet permits the naturally gifted this special licence to play.

And she did it all with a wonderful lack of calculation. Deauville bikinis are small and often notional, and postures relaxed to the point of abandonment. But it must follow, given the caprices of anatomy, that hundreds of hours must be spent in bedrooms and bathrooms in patient finicking – because with the single exception of this girl, I saw not one woman betray so much as a trace of pubic hair.

What about the people I know? What would they make of it? About Penny, I've not a moment's doubt : she'd wander topless without a bashful flicker. She'd have done so when twenty ; she'd do it now ; and for all I know will be doing it twenty years hence. What about Evie? It seems absurd, but I haven't a clue. Neither about her nor Beeb. Among friends perhaps, but in a public place I just don't know.

And Ess ; what about her? Persephone was right about her, I'm fairly sure. She'd have liked the idea of being modern ; but when it came to unhitching herself, disabling qualms would have intervened. She would have found herself demanding a greater illusion of privacy than even that strange beach allows.

Jimmy and Beeb have had a card from Boomer. He's in New Jersey and convalescing well.

After supper, I discovered that Beeb and Evie share a theory of dislocation. According to this, the relation of man to woman is doomed eternally to flip-flop. No sooner has the man established himself as down-to-earth, and the woman established herself as romantic than there's a reversal, and it's the woman who's preoccupied with the carnal, while the man is off in the clouds. The romantic and the carnal, then: two systems of imaginative comprehension, oscillating for all eternity out of phase.

A more prosaic item of their joint wisdom is that husbands who give value in bed are not forced by their wives to shop or cook against their inclination. (It follows that Beeb must have made more of that distressing conversation around Penny's supper-table than I'd imagined — the one about men coping in the kitchen. She was pouring oil and binding wounds, but at the same time, presumably, putting two and two together. Among others, about Perce.) Detecting feminism, I cited the unsatisfactory heroine of 'The Man in the Brooks Brothers Shirt': her conjugal tendernesses that were brightly packaged substitutes for the 'real thing'. For the 'long carnal swoon' that she could never quite execute in the marriage bed. But they were unimpressed. Evie was emphatic that only an American academic would attempt to *execute* a long carnal swoon, while Beeb thinks that longing for the real thing is a disease that afflicts both sexes alike. Swoons are more like flashes of lightning. An accident of nature, and somewhat rare.

A muddled conversation. I looked across to see what Jimmy was making of it, but he was staring out of the window at the black shadows cast by the sycamore, its leaves coated in greenfly and sticky in the way that sycamores are towards the end of a long summer.

October 30th

Sometime in the last month, Evie and I almost got married. Almost but not quite. There was nothing to stop us but a kernel of hope. Unfortunately, that proved lacking. To launch anything as profoundly speculative, you need an upwelling of some sort : if not of hope, at least of animal high-spirits that you can mistake for hope. But none occurred. With Evie, there are no prospects of hillsides sparkling with buttercups in the adman's summer light. On the contrary, people in her imagination always seem to die. Although she has none of Penny's capacity for devastation, it's the aftermath of carnage that love-making seems to press upon her.

Beeb approved : she said as much while we were washing up together after supper. And we nearly made it. But we could not suspend disbelief; it was a scheme shot through with flaws.

November 11th

As usual, I've tried to bury disappointment under a

mountain of numbers, but the events of the last few months keep rearranging themselves in my dreams — ones in which Evie's moguls appear and reappear, strangely foetal creatures, awash in an amniotic sea of cash. By day, though, I've been giving what I believe is a competent impersonation of a Protestant accumulator. My masters have noticed nothing, and seem pleased.

November 12th

What deaths leave behind them — Ess's, even Perce's — is the sense of a three-dimensional array gradually flattening itself into two dimensions. Of familiar figures surrounded by the air we all breathe flattening themselves out into a picture.

What Boomer's departure has left behind in Penny's mind turns out to be unaffected astonishment. He pushed off without telling her, and she just can't believe it.

November 14th

The year's running out in dribs and drabs. I can feel it. For months now, we're doomed to live in inverted commas, at one remove.

November 17th

I'd planned a restorative supper with Penny at Bertorelli's, but she called it off at the last moment. She says she's ill, but is probably just depressed. Either way, it's new ground for the two of us: she's never admitted to me before that she feels feeble or unable to cope. Certainly, she's lost weight. She looked dried, almost shrivelled.

Having an empty freezer, I decided to go anyway and eat on my own. I'd have liked to ring Jimmy, but there's now a tiresome awkwardness between us — the worst hazard of attachment among the middle-aged. Each spasm of hope loses you more old friends.

At the next table, a well-known Swedish director, female, whose name I still can't remember, was locked in conversation with a man twenty years her junior. I spent some time trying to work out whether their topic was work or love, disguising my efforts with carefully timed sips and mouthfuls.

Their air of mutual preoccupation distracted me from what I would otherwise have noticed at once: Boomer, with his back to me, half-hidden, on the far side of the room. I'd assumed that he was safely tucked up, four thousand miles away, on the other side of the Atlantic. I was already out of my chair to say hello when I noticed that the woman with him was Beeb. She had reached a notable arm across the tablecloth and, amidst the plates and cutlery, was holding him tightly by the hand. Like the film director and her young man, they were totally absorbed.

Rattled, I paid up and bolted. What were they talking about? Penny and her outrages? Ess? I don't think so. There was something dogged about the set of his head, and on his face an expression of half-resolved confusion. I suspect that, at last, he's found an audience worthy of his stories about the *Scharnhorst* and the evil young Hogg: someone able to mirror for him their hidden meaning.

In the hours since, I have been sifting for the clues

142

that ought to have alerted me to a rift between Beeb and Jimmy; to a growth of sympathy between Beeb and Boomer the Bereft. They were there, but I misread them. Boomer and Beeb: the two Bs. For the moment, it's more than I can get my mind round. And who's to cook for Jimmy? In the short term, it'll have to be Evie. In the long, who knows?

The time has come to abandon all effort and allow the absorbent wadding of televised sport to do it's work. I'll remain comatose until the first breath of spring air. In March, the sun will show through waterily, literary snippets will crop up like crocuses, and the cycle will begin all over again. The urge to know what you can never quite know. To know and to 'know'. But in mid-November, you feel like a field that can't lie fallow. The victim of some artful scheme of crop rotation, you'd rather be back with the gorse and the brambles.

To bide me over, I'll get a video attachment for my Telefunken, my only beautiful possession, and play un-ending loops to myself each evening of Sonia Lannaman winning the 200 metres. Sonia Lannaman and Sharon Colyear. Loops that I can run forward, run back and freeze. And through the headphones, who? Again black — Gonzalves's tenor. The pure and impure, spun together into that single silken thread.